I0544175

Love is for Suckers

REBEL WILD

Love is for Suckers

Copyright © 2023 by Rebel Wild

All rights reserved. This book or any portion thereof may not be reproduced or used in any manner whatsoever without the express written permission of the publisher except for the use of brief quotations in a book review.

This is a work of fiction. Names, characters, businesses, places, events, locales, and incidents are either the products of the author's imagination or used in a fictitious manner. Any resemblance to actual persons, living or dead, or actual events is purely coincidental.

Printed in the United States of America
First Printing, 2023

Cover Design by Vanilla Lily Designs Company
Interior formatting by Alt 19 Creative

www.rebelwildbooks.com

Dedicated to Matthew for keeping me laughing throughout this entire process.

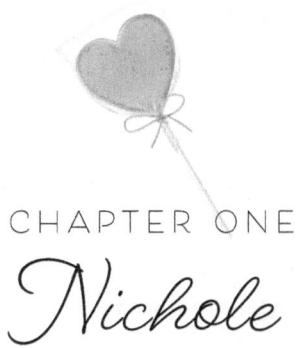

CHAPTER ONE

Nichole

FEBRUARY 1

THE SLAMMING of the front door to my duplex apartment startles me. I turn the TV off to listen for the footsteps. I'm trying to decide if I should stay in bed or make a run for it. I don't have a baseball bat or anything in here. I don't know why I agreed to move out of the Alpha Psi sorority house. At least there was a huge security door standing between me and any possible killer. Luckily, I hear heels stomping on the hardwood floor. I would know the sound of that walk anywhere.

"Dericka, is that you?" I yell through my closed door just to make sure it's my roommate and bestie, Dericka Andrews.

"No, I'm a demented killer coming to stab you with my stilettos."

"Bitch."

"Of course, it's me," she says, coming in.

"You're back early. How was your hook-up with Shawn?" Her flopping down on my bed is answer enough. "That bad, huh?"

"He barely lasted. Girl, that asshole spent the whole night revving me up, getting me all excited, but when it came time to handle his business he tapped out after five damn minutes."

"Ouch," I say, shaking my hand like it's been burned. "Well, did he do other things after he was done?" She shakes her head. "No licking, no fingering… nothing?"

"He passed out."

"Aw, that sucks."

"I know, right? So, I got myself off, used up all his shower gel, and left his ass sleeping. I even took his toilet paper so he'll have to do the walk of shame when he takes his first shit in the morning."

"That's right."

"How was your date with Terrence? Tell me *he* didn't suck."

"I'm sitting here on the computer, already in pajamas with my bonnet on my head, aren't I? I've been home for hours."

"You're kidding? Him too?"

"At least Shawn gave you a few strokes. Terrence came all over his own damn hands and all I was doing was taking off my bra." She howls with laughter. "It's not *that* funny, Dericka."

"It's hilarious. I told you your boobs are like weapons. They bring men to their knees. Or in Terrence's case, to his pre-ejaculation." She laughs again.

"Shut up!" I smack her leg with the back of my hand. "And so much for Valentine's Day. After that performance, I told him to find another loser to take out. I really wanted to go to that concert too. Looks like I'm going to be playing with myself on the one day of the year made for love."

"Love is for suckers, but we still need good dick."

"You'd think somebody on campus would have one as much as they all brag about it."

"They lie. Trust me. I've fucked more than half of them and they don't got shit."

"It figures."

"You know what? That's it." She slaps her palm on the bed. "I'm done with college boys. I'm going outside the realm to find a *real* man. Someone that can hang with me."

"Who's to say they get better with age?"

"Every damn romance book I've read on the subject. Why do you think so many young girls go for the older guys?"

"Money. Look at that zillionaire sports team owner guy. He's almost a hundred and still has girls all over him. You *know* it's his money. You really want to deal with some guy's shriveled-up old dick?"

"I said *older,* not ancient."

"Okay, true." I concede her point, typing in a search for LA's hottest guys over thirty. "Wow, take a look at him." I show her the screen shot of Earth's Best Chocolate's CEO.

"He's number one. I've been drooling over his chocolate cake commercials all week now."

"Gredin McEwen," she says. "He's hot, but unfortunately he's married."

"How do you know?"

"Because I live in the world. The man is loaded and he makes chocolate for a living. He has to have a woman stashed away somewhere."

"Well, he's with this chick with one of his jawbreakers in her mouth." I show her the picture with him eye fucking some blonde. They're coming out of a club and it looks like she just stopped to pose for the camera.

"That's probably her. Who else would take that stupid picture? She's definitely pimping her man's candy."

"He doesn't have a ring on his finger."

"That don't mean shit. He could just be private. Which is a good thing. Who wants everyone in your business anyway?"

"True."

"You should find out."

"How?"

"Go after him."

She gets up to take her clothes off. I roll my eyes when she climbs under my covers without so much as underwear on.

"Like I can just stroll up to him and ask."

"Why not?"

"And say what?"

"Be direct."

"Yeah, I can just see it now, 'Hi, I'm Nichole and I need to get laid by a *real* man so why don't we go to your place and you can do me.' That would go over real well."

"It should. You're hot. Why not go for it?"

"Because it's a sure way to get me manhandled by his security team."

I slide my laptop over so she can see him surrounded by his entourage.

"Works for me," she says, checking them all out.

"You're such a whore," I say, closing the lid and putting it on the floor next to my bed. I slide down, turning away from her so I can get some sleep. I blow out an annoyed breath when I feel her hand creeping up my leg. "No," I tell her, squashing her hopes of doing it with me tonight.

"C'mon, Nik."

"Not tonight, Dericka."

"You're such a damn prude, *Nichole*."

BEING RUDELY woken up by the sound of laughing, I pull the covers over my head to go back to sleep.

"Oh, no you don't. Wake your ass up before you're late for class. You don't want to keep Professor Hottie waiting."

"He's *your* hottie, not mine. He looks like Big Bird to me and what's so damn funny at seven in the morning?"

"Shawn texted saying he had the night of his life. I guess he enjoyed his party of one."

I laugh getting out of bed, going to the shower.

"I really hope they take it easy on us today. I'm not in the mood to do any work."

"We can always blow off class and head to the beach," she says.

"I want to save that for a better day."

"I'm all for that," she says.

"Dull day on campus, here we come."

When my high school guidance counselor told me to apply for an art scholarship at UCLA, I thought she was nuts. Don't get me wrong, I knew I had the grades and even the talent, but I also knew it was competitive as hell. Besides the fact that I had my heart set on Alabama State since it was my mom's alma mater. I applied on a whim only to get my counselor off my back about it. No one was more surprised than me when I got in.

Now, here I am, a small-town country girl in LA bitching about not wanting to do school work in a college that rich kids cheat to get into. What can I say? I guess I'm living the life.

SO MUCH for taking it easy today. I had two pop quizzes and a short essay on Pablo Picasso's blue period. Skipping my last class, I grab some lunch in the café before calling it a day and heading home.

A car is double parked waiting for a space to open up and I'm about to make the guy's day. I see him checking me out as I pass between his car and mine. He's hot. I wouldn't mind giving him my number if he asked. I click the key to unlock my doors.

"You leaving?" He's talking more to my tits than to me.

I think he's on the basketball team, but so is Terrence and we all know how that turned out. I'll pass on this one.

"Yep," I say, shifting my backpack so I can open my door. Of course, the damn thing slips off my shoulder and I have to catch it before it falls on the ground.

"Need some help with that?"

"I'm good," I say before getting in.

I forgot to leave my windows cracked so it's sweltering in here. I let them all down before turning on my engine. Since he needs the spot, I don't bother letting the car warm up a little like I normally do. I throw it in reverse and wait until he backs up enough to let me out. The garage isn't that packed with cars trying to leave, thank God. It usually takes me ten minutes just to get out of the parking garage at the end of the day.

San Vicente Blvd. on the other hand is bumper to bumper. Where are they all going this time of day and don't they have jobs? It's times like these that make me miss home. Out in the country where we lived, I could drive for miles without passing another car or even being stopped by a traffic light. When I first learned how to drive, I would fly up and down the highway. I never felt so free. Here I'm rushing from one traffic light to the next with people who are going nowhere fast.

I pull into my driveway just in time to wave goodbye to my neighbor as she pulls out. She owns the place. She's an older lady but doesn't mind renting to us as long as we keep the noise down. Dericka promised her we'd be like two little church mice. So far, we've been good, but she's dying to throw a party.

I feel my backpack for my house keys as I walk up the front steps. I was never allowed to keep my car and house keys on the same ring. It was a pet peeve of my grandfather's. If I lost the one ring, he'd have to replace all the keys. I hope they're not buried at the bottom because I don't want to take everything out. I don't have to worry about it because I see Dericka at the door.

"Guess what?" she asks, pulling it open for me.

"Thanks for the save," I say. I'm wondering why she's not moving to let me in.

"Are you going to guess?"

"Oh, um... you didn't go to your last class today either. How you're maintaining that high GPA is a mystery to me."

"I work with what my momma gave me, boo boo," she says, shaking her ass.

I smack it out of my way before I walk by her.

"Guess who agreed to donate a brand-new Rolex for our online auction this year? Which is definitely going to put us over the top, by the way. Those skank ass Kappa Gamma bitches aren't going to get anything in the vicinity of a damn Rolex."

"You know this is for charity, right?"

"I still want to win. A trip to Cancun is up for grabs and are you going to guess, or what?"

"I don't know. Some rich person."

"Oh, my God, bitch, *really*?"

"Just tell me already."

"Okay." She takes a deep breath. "It's the hottest, possibly married, CEO himself. Mr. Candy."

"No. You're kidding?"

"And guess who has the paperwork for him to sign?"

"You?"

"I was at Alpha Psi when it came in. I took that shit before anyone else saw it."

"I hate you."

"Well, now you're going to love me because I'm passing it on to you. Make sure he signs the part where we can use a picture of him on the website. Maybe some other rich guy will see it and try to upstage him. You know how they like to brag about all the underprivileged people their money is helping. Meanwhile, they pay their employees like crap. Is a livable wage too much to ask for? Talk about a big issue."

"Can we focus on *my* issue, please? How am I going to find out if he's available? I just can't come right out and ask."

"Wing it," she shrugs, handing me the paperwork.

"Why are you giving me this now?"

"Because the memo said he can only sign it today at five."

"What!"

"He's on a cake-making deadline or some shit."

"Oh, my God."

"Yep, and it's Friday so you know the traffic downtown is *terrible*. You better get a move on."

"What am I going to wear?" I say, dragging my jeans and hoodie off.

"I know the perfect outfit," she assures me as I hop in the shower.

"I LOOK easy," I tell her. I'm wearing the crimson red dress I bought for my homecoming dance back in high school. I don't know how she found the damn thing. I buried it in the back of my closet. She matched it with sky-high heels. "It's business at the bottom," I say, looking at the knee length, but it's all slut at the top." My tits are pushed so high up they're choking me. They definitely weren't this big in high school or my grandmother would have never let me wear this dress.

"That's the point. You look professionally hot, but still not against opening your legs." I have to agree with her. I *do* look hot. I don't know about the legs part. She slaps some red lipstick on me because she says it brings out my eyes. I don't know how red brings out brown eyes but I go with it. "Okay," she says as she pushes me toward the door. "Be sure to flash those tits. It's your way into his bed. Trust me."

"Right," I say grabbing my bag and my keys.

"And don't forget to bring back a souvenir so I can envy you properly. His undies will do. I wonder if he's a briefs man. He looks like a briefs man."

"I'll let you know."

"You go, girl!"

She swats my ass out the door.

CHAPTER TWO

Nichole

DRIVE DOWN San Vicente to Wilshire but before I hit the 405 freeway, I put the windows up and the AC on to keep my jet-black hair from flying away. It's long and parted down the middle, but not too straight. That will make it easy to fix if I mess it up by having wild sex.

I check my phone when I reach my destination and it's fifteen minutes to five. I still have to find parking. I know I'm not going to make it on time. I hate being late. Fate is on my side because there's a parking lot with vacancies right across the street and I give the guy fifty bucks to park. He must see how desperate I am, but I don't have time to bitch to him about overcharging me. Running so I can make the light, I cross over to Persian Square.

I enter the McEwen corporate office building. There's a huge chocolate fountain in the center of the lobby. I know it's not real chocolate because it doesn't smell like it, but it's psyching me out and I want to stick my finger in and taste it. The walls are dusky pink with teal accents and wherever they can get away with it, there's some type of candy as a theme. It's like the *Candyland* board game come to life. I'm half expecting to see *Lord Licorice* and *Princess Lolly* go skipping by.

I pep myself up all the way over to the front desk, giving her my full name and waiting for permission to move forward. Then I pep myself up again as I follow the directions to his office. I can't help but notice how thin everyone is here. I bet it's because they can't stand chocolate. I'd probably hate it if I had to look at it this much. I hope it hasn't turned him off of black girls because *this* black girl is about to rock his world.

After a quick knock on his door, a deep, rich voice tells me to come in. It has me wondering if the energy of the man matches the baritone.

"Miss Nichole Adams, welcome," he says a

He comes from behind his desk to shake my hand.

Shit, he's even hotter in person. And thank you, Jesus, he's tall which is a good thing since I'm five-eight.

"Oh," I say, catching myself. I shake the hand he's still offering me. "Nice to meet you, Mr. McEwen. Thank you for seeing me on such short notice."

"I owed it to your chancellor. Please, have a seat."

"Thank you." I take the seat right in front of his desk where he'll have the best view of me.

"I'm afraid I'm on a tight schedule, so if you can keep it brief."

"Of course, I completely understand," I say, clearing my throat dramatically and pretending to cough a little. I hope he takes the bait.

"Would you like something to drink?" he says, on his way back to his desk.

Score!

He was raised with manners. That's a plus.

"Wine would be lovely if you have it."

"Wine." He stops in his tracks to look at me.

"I'm a little wound up from the drive. The freeway traffic was stop-and-go."

"Of course." He calls who I'm guessing is his assistant and rattles off some European-sounding name of a wine I've never heard of. "How does that sound?" he says to me after he hangs up the phone.

"Excellent. Thank you." I know nothing about wine, but my obsessing over his pictures yesterday showed him drinking a lot of it. Evidently, it pairs well with his chocolate. "I'll just let you get started reading over these." I slide him the forms. "I don't want to keep you."

"Let's wait for the wine. I can spare a few more minutes. So, you're a member of Alpha Psi? I'm familiar with that sorority. What made you pledge?"

Damn. Is he sizing me up? He's a boardroom CEO at his finest. Okay, how do I play this? Alpha Psi is known for its high moral stance, which is why I joined. They call us the nuns of sorority row. But do I tell him the truth, or lie and give him some song and dance about using them to advance my career? I get the feeling that "good girls" aren't his forte and that's the last thing I want him to think I am. Unless, of course, he has some kink about fucking one and that can definitely work in my favor.

Which way do I go? I cross my fingers that I play this right.

"Okay," I start, looking guilty cute. Guys love that stuff. "I have a confession. I'm not *that* into sorority life. I don't even live there. I'm an art major and what kind of living am I going to make out of that, right? You kick over a trashcan and a starving artist comes crawling out. Everyone knows belonging to a sorority is an asset, so I figured I'd aim high when I pledged. Alpha Psi is the best, but I never thought they'd let a person like me in."

"A person like you?"

"I'm no angel."

I hope that sounded as flirty as I meant it to. I wait and gauge his reaction. This could *so* backfire. Damn, I should have just stuck with the truth.

Don't start doubting yourself now. You can still pull out of this.

"Devils have more fun." He says it with a smirk.

Ha! Jackpot.

"I can't disagree."

"What's your form of art?"

"Painting. Anything erotic or perverse."

"I wouldn't have thought that would ignite your passion?" He chuckles. "I was thinking something more along the lines of couples in a sweet embrace or pretty ponies and kittens."

"Is *that* what you think art is? That's way too boring. I'm into the more basic levels of human nature."

"Basic levels?"

"Humans were once wild animals. We've become much too domesticated, like those kittens you speak of. Which is why I'm drawn more to perversion. I prefer the rough and not the fluff."

"*Ahem*, I see," he says, loosening his tie. "It's one thing to enjoy it in a painting, but how does it transfer over to human relationships— this *animalistic* behavior?"

I stifle a laugh.

"You're giving off images of two dogs stuck together in heat."

"I suppose you can't get any more basic than that," he says, with a lift of his eyebrows.

The air in here is so charged the little hairs on the back of my neck are standing up. I'm trying hard not to squirm at the turn of this conversation. How did we get on this?

Shit, he's eye-fucking me. I better play up my assets.

I shift in my chair so that my dress raises a little too high up my thigh while I stick my chest out. His dark eyes roam over me and I can just make out the tip of his tongue as he tries not to lick his lips.

I have his attention but I have no clue what to do next. The boys I know are usually all over me by now. I'm way out of my league here.

He's about to speak when his assistant comes in with our wine, giving me a chance to regroup. He looks annoyed at her but says nothing as she sets down the glasses.

"Thank you," I say to her when she's done, and she nods.

"See to it that we're not disturbed," he tells her rather abruptly.

"Certainly, Mr. McEwen," she says, leaving us alone.

He hands me my glass and I nearly drop it from the shock of our hands touching. Judging by the way he's looking at me I know he felt it too.

I take a long sip before I put it down. I need liquid courage.

"Thank you for the wine and the conversation, but I'm sure you have better things to do than play around with me."

"I'm feeling rather playful at the moment. Fortunately for you."

"For me?"

"Let's just say not many can handle my animalistic instincts."

"I'm not one of the many, Mr. McEwen."

"Perhaps you'll be one of my select few."

"You should be so blessed."

"Faith does favor the brave."

"I thought it was fortune."

"That too."

He starts to read over the paperwork, rolling the pen between his long fingers. I can't help but notice how skilled he is at doing that. I wonder what else he can do with those fingers. He flips the page and I look around, searching for something to say to prolong my stay. Coming up empty, I go for the obvious.

"How did you get into candy of all things?"

"What's wrong with candy?"

"Nothing at all. I love it. I'm just curious as to what got you interested in the business of making it as opposed to venturing into automotive or corporate raiding."

He looks at me, smiles, then leans back in his chair, seemingly tired of being asked the question, but I know better. Score another one for me.

He rattles out the standardly shallow answer I've heard him give in a few interviews I've watched as I sip more wine. Even though I know he's full of shit, I can't keep my eyes off him. Never have I been so entranced by watching a man talk. I imagine that mouth of his sucking on different parts of me.

His dark brown hair is a little long at the top and a strand of it falls like a superman curl in the middle of his forehead. I'm hypnotized by it until he rakes it back with his hand breaking the spell.

He stops, and leans forward, smirking at catching me staring.

"Interesting," I say, not having a clue as to what his answer was.

"Was it?" He challenges me while tossing his pen on his desk. I nod before taking another sip from my glass. "So, you heard all of that while you were checking me out?"

I choke on my wine. He rushes over and takes the glass, ready to pat me on the back if I choke again.

"I'm very good at multitasking, Mr. McEwen." I resist

the urge to cough up the wine still stuck in my windpipe. Instead, I take the glass from him and gulp more down.

"Obviously not very good at *swallowing*, Miss Andrews."

"It all depends on what's in my mouth, Mr. McEwen. Do you have a habit of underestimating all women or is it just something about me?"

"I give credit to any woman who can get me to rise to the occasion."

"And how many can do that?"

"As I've said, it's a select few. Blame my animal instinct."

"Are you saying you like to devour your women like prey?"

"Is knowing that a requirement for your sorority's auction or is this a *personal* curiosity?"

"My sorority most definitely wouldn't look favorably upon me mentioning it, so consider it personal. Speaking of personal, are you married to that woman in the picture with the jawbreaker in her mouth?"

The temperature in the room drops by a few thousand degrees and I know I just blew it.

"What about this song and dance we've been doing would make you think so?" he spits at me.

"I apologize— "

"Does your sorority make it a habit of being so invasive? If so, I don't think I want to participate in your auction."

"No, I'm... as I said it was personal. I just..." I try to backtrack, but he's lifting me by the arm out of my seat. He lets me go so he can grab his phone. "Who are you calling?"

"My security. I'm having your ass tossed out of here."

"Wait, Mr. McEwen, it's not what you think."

"Then what the hell is it?"

"I... okay, confession time..."

"Spit it out."

"Okay. Alpha Psi doesn't know I'm here. See, my room-mate, Dericka and I... we... well, we get bored and she's into sex and she kind of got me into it, but I haven't had as much experience as she's had. She and I fool around, but when it comes to boys, well, my first time was awful. I mean, I didn't really get to *do* anything. He ended up spilling out in his hands before I could even get my clothes off. So, I'm still a virgin. But then, I saw your picture on the internet and I thought you looked hot, and then my stupid roommate gave me the forms for you to sign. She thought maybe I'd be able to seduce you into bed. It was very stupid of me to try. I do apologize and you don't have to call security. I'll just go. I only ask that you not tell the chancellor about any of this. I don't want to get expelled."

"You're a *virgin*." He projects the last word out of his mouth in shock. You have *got* to be kidding me. I just spilled my guts and that's all he heard. That I'm a virgin. Bad enough Dericka gives me shit about it, now I have to hear it from him too. No thank you. "You came here so I can fuck you?"

"I can see what an awful mistake it was. It was a dumb thing to do and I'm completely embarrassed. Honestly, I'm mortified. I'll send someone else to pick up the forms and the watch. Please, don't hold this against the charity. It's for a really good cause—"

"Stop talking."

"I… okay, I'll shut up. I'll just be on my way."

I turn to make a run for it before he has me hauled out of here, but he's across the room with me pressed up to the door so fast I nearly faint from my head spinning.

"There's no way in hell you're leaving."

"There's not?"

"No," he whispers. "Unless we're done here, but I hope you stay and allow me the pleasure of being the first to fuck you."

"But I thought I pissed you off."

"I'm over it."

"You're a very hard man to follow."

"And you're a very tempting woman. But this will be just a fuck-and-done—a one-time thing. Is this really how you want to lose your virginity?"

"I wouldn't want it any other way."

His mouth crashes into mine. The kiss is rough but controlled. He pushes my dress up over my ass and lifts me in his arms. My legs instinctively wrap around him. I'm deposited on his desk. He reaches around and with one swoop of his hand, the contents go flying across the floor. His hands are at the back of my dress, unzipping it.

"Mmm." His low growl at the sight of my tits gets me wet.

I moan as his hands make their way into my panties.

"Fuck," he hisses. "You're already so wet, Miss Adams, I like that."

He slides my dress and panties off so smoothly it leaves me breathless. He pushes me back farther and I slide in my own juices. My back hits the cold wood as he presses me down on the desk. I watch as he goes around and takes something out of his drawer. It's not until the metal clamps around my wrists that I realize it's handcuffs.

"To satisfy the animal in me," he says.

"Ah," I moan when his mouth is suddenly at my clit. I didn't even realize he'd moved.

No one but Dericka has ever done this to me before and he puts her to shame. I come quickly, like I always do, and he licks up my juices.

"You taste divine. Even better than I imagined you would."

I watch with hooded eyes as he tears a condom wrapper and slides it on. He runs his dick up and down my pussy, making me squirm at the pressure of it on my now overly-stimulated clit.

"I want this," I whisper when he hesitates.

He grabs me by the hips and thrusts into me. I cry out in pain as his dick has just opened me up wide. He stills himself inside me.

"Relax." His voice is low and husky with desire for me. "Fuck," he says as he thrust gently into me. I can't help but contract around him. I grip the edge of the desk above me with my cuffed hands to steady myself as his thrusts get harder. He has one of my thighs in his hand, wrapping my leg around his waist. "You like this, Miss Adams?"

"Yes."

"Mmm, that's right," he says as I move faster.

He raises both of my legs and rests them on his shoulders. The sides of my heels are pressed against both his ears. My grunting fills the room as he hammers hard into me over and over and over again. I feel myself building and I'm unable to stop it. He has total control over me.

"Oh, God," I scream as I come.

I buck and squirm as I ride through it. I come down just in time to witness him fall apart above me, calling my name as he comes.

"Shit," he pants, falling back into the chair behind him. I don't know how long I lay there basking in the afterglow of my first fuck before I feel him undo the handcuffs. "Was that perverse enough for your liking?"

"It was perfect."

I TRY to get up but my legs are wobbly so he has to help me get dressed again. I tie my hair back in a low ponytail and I don't even know if my lipstick is still on but I press my lips together to fix it anyway. He's staring at me the whole time. I'm starting to feel a little self-conscious.

"Have dinner with me tonight?" he finally says. "I hate to leave it like this. I want to make sure you're okay."

He signs the forms without even reading the last few pages and hands them to me.

"I'm fine and that goes against the whole fuck-and-done thing we agreed on."

He nods in concession before going around his desk to get the Rolex. I half-ass wonder what else he has stashed away in that drawer.

"Thanks a lot," I say, taking the watch.

I chance a kiss on his cheek before I walk out the door, but I stop short, remembering something.

"Miss Adams?"

"There's just one last thing I need."

"WELL, THANK you again for the donation, Mr. McEwen," I say formally as we pass the reception desk in a bad attempt to save face.

"It was my pleasure, believe me," he teases and I want to sock him out.

We wait awkwardly at the elevator. His assistant is eyeing us suspiciously and I try hard not to wonder whether or not she knows anything. I bet she heard me. I know I was loud. Whatever. I'm not going to care. I don't even have to see her again after today.

I breathe a sigh of relief when the elevator doors open and I step in. I give a little wave to him as the doors close and he nods, grinning like he just ate the canary.

Love is for Suckers

I SLUMP back, exhausted as I ride down to the first floor. I'm going to have a lot to say to Father Tolan this week at confessional. Would it be a sin if I didn't tell him? God already knows. Why do I have to tell Father Tolan? It's none of his damn business.

Great. I've just committed a carnal sin and now I'm being disrespectful to my priest. I'm going to hell for sure.

Despite that fact, I still can't help but laugh. I have *the* Gredin McEwen's black boxer briefs he gave me as a souvenir in my bag. I twirl the handcuffs he never took back around my index finger, full of myself, as I walk out of the building, gasping when I realize I don't have my panties. He never put them back on me.

Well played, Mr. McEwen. Well played.

CHAPTER THREE

Nichole

I PRAY MY legs can take me back to my car without giving out. My heart is racing and I don't know if this is normal, but between my legs feels weird. Like I've been stretched out of shape or like he still should be inside me to fill the hole he left. I can't explain it, but my vaginal wall keeps contracting like it's wondering where he went.

Hugging myself, I cross the street. I can't even look the people I'm passing in the intersection in the eye. I feel like they know what I just did.

Even though there's a slight breeze, I feel the heat of embarrassment radiating just underneath my skin. I keep my head down and count the cracks in the pavement.

Hopping in my car, I breathe a sigh of relief. I flip my visor down, getting a look in the mirror. I don't know if I should be pleased with myself or thoroughly disgusted. I snap it back up with a stupid grin on my face because who am I kidding? I'm *so* pleased with myself. If "mission accomplished" was a person it would definitely be me.

My hands are shaking with so much excitement, I can barely put the key in the ignition. I take a minute to calm down enough to drive.

I COME home to an eager Dericka. She's walking a groove in the living room floor with her bare, freshly manicured feet. Her blonde highlighted passion-twisted hair is wrapped in a bun and she has her pink polka dot pajamas on. She's the picture of college life.

"Well?" She demands answers as soon as I walk in. She has her foot stuck out, tapping it like my grandmother used to do when I came home a minute late. Being five foot ten, Dericka is way more intimidating when she does it. "You were *supposed* to call me." Her bitchiness is on full display.

"Sorry, that part completely slipped my mind," I say with a guilty grimace followed by my own I-just-ate-the-canary grin.

I'm still riding the high from having been fucked by Gredin McEwen. My body's whizzing through space at warp speed, factor: Thoroughly Fucked.

"What the hell happened? Did it work? I'm guessing it worked. I'm guessing something good happened the way you're grinning at me right now."

"Something *totally* happened."

"What? What the hell happened?"

"*It* happened, Dericka. It *totally* happened."

"Get out!" She squeals, taking my hand and pulling me down on the couch next to her. "Tell me. Tell me."

"On his desk. In his office." I dig through my bag, pulling stuff out. "Handcuffs," I say, holding them up, and showing them off. "And… and… these babies."

"No damn way," she says, trying to snatch Gredin's boxer briefs from me.

"No, you don't," I say, putting them back in my bag. "Those are all mine. You can have this." I hand her the forms he signed and the Rolex.

"I hate you," she says, tossing them on the coffee table. "At least give me details. Please tell me he wasn't another pre-comer like Terrence. Was he at least as hot in person as he is on the internet? Was *it* hot? Did he get you to come?"

"He's all hotness and oh, my God, Dericka, I'm so glad I didn't give it up to Terrence. Gredin made my whole body sing. He played me like a fiddle. I came! I came so damn hard, I almost passed out."

"Oh, my God," she shrills, falling over with laughter. "I knew it. I *knew* older guys were the way to go. We have to find me one. We can't let another Valentine's Day go by with me hanging out with my dildo."

"We're on it. Operation: Get Dericka Fucked by Older Sex God, starts tomorrow."

"First thing," she says, holding out her pinky. I circle it with mine so I can pinky promise with her.

"WHELP," I say getting up, about ready to call this thing a day.

My body is sore and all I want to do is hop in the shower, get a bowl of ice cream, drink some wine if we even have any because I like it now, and go to bed.

"Where the hell do you think you're going?" she asks.

"To shower."

"You fucked and haven't showered?" She looks me up and down.

"Where the heck was I supposed to shower?"

"Did he eat you out?"

"Mm-hm."

"So, he's like still all up in you?"

"Sort of. His saliva is, I guess. He used a condom when we fucked though. So... shower," I say, turning to leave.

"Not yet." She pulls me back down on the couch. "I want to taste how he tastes all over you."

"You have *got* to be kidding. You're a goddamn pervert, Dericka Andrews."

"And you love benefiting from it. 'Oh, Dericka, oh God, right there,'" she says, mocking me.

"Shut up," I squeal, hitting her with a throw pillow. "I do *not* sound like *that*."

"Whatever helps you come," she says, pulling my dress up over my waist. "Where are your panties?"

"Um..." I try to concentrate enough to remember where they are but her breath's just inches away from my already wet pussy making it hard. "Gredin still has them, I think... mmm..." I try to talk but her thumb is circling my clit, sliding over the slickness that Gredin left with little effort.

"You're still bleeding," she says.

"Really?" I lift to see but she grabs hold of my tit, pushing me back down.

"I got this," she says, rubbing my clit faster.

She knows just the right amount of pressure it takes to drive me nuts.

"Oh, God," I moan deeply when her tongue plunges into my pussy, trying to taste what's left of the cum I gave to Gredin.

"You like that?"

She soon slips the long nail of her middle finger inside me. She hooks it to hit my g spot and I buck off the couch. My insides start to shake as every nerve ending meets up between my legs. I am seconds away from coming.

"Yes," I whisper to her. I take hold of her head. My nails dig into her scalp, making sure she doesn't move. Her tongue is flicking my clit and her finger is fucking me as I grind my pussy into her face. "Shit," I whisper as I come. I mewl around when I'm done, letting her continue to lick me.

"Damn, I love it when you come."

"Yeah, and you're too good at getting me to do it. For a dick lover, you sure know how to eat my pussy."

"I like the taste." She holds her finger with my cum mixed with blood on it to my mouth.

"Yeah, well I don't," I say, moving my head away, grossed out.

"Lucky for you it tastes even better after you've fucked a guy, especially for the first time." She sucks it off her fingernail. I hide my face with my hands, shaking my head. "I can't believe you still get embarrassed about this shit."

"It's not like I've done this stuff before I met you. I'm Catholic, you know. I went to schools *literally* run by nuns."

"You're certainly making up for lost time. You just banged, as far as the public knows, the very un-bangable Gredin McEwen. So much for the married rumor. He's not, is he?"

"No, he's not. I wouldn't have done it if he was. I almost got in trouble for asking him about that jawbreaker chick, by the way. He was going to have me thrown out and expelled. He was so pissed."

"What stopped him?"

"I told him about my crazy ass roommate, you, and the plan she hatched up to get her virgin roommate, me, laid by a man with experience, him, that I was crushing on over the internet."

"I bet he ate that virgin part up."

"Yes, he did."

"What a silly thing to get mad about. There has to be a story there."

"Probably his ex. I'll tell you one thing; she was stupid to let him go. He is big."

"How big?"

"You remember that Mandingo porn we watched?"

"Shut the fuck up. *That* big?"

"Mm-hm."

"Shit. I wonder if he has a brother?"

"Don't know."

"Ask him."

"I'm never going to talk to him again."

"You don't want to see him again for sure, because I'll lose these forms so you can go back for round two?"

"The sisters would kill you. They'd probably kick you out of the sorority."

"I'd deal."

"You would do that for me?"

"Hell yeah. I would bite that bullet for my bestie in a New York minute."

"You're the best bestie *ever.*"

"So, it's on?"

"Nope, not going to happen."

"Maybe he wants to see you."

"He wanted to take me out to dinner to make sure I was okay—"

"And you didn't say yes?"

"There was no point. I was okay and it was a one-time thing. Plus, it's less messy this way."

"Uh-huh."

"I mean it. I did what I wanted to do and experienced what I wanted to experience. Now that I know what all the fuss is about, I'm moving on to something else."

"What else is there? Sex is it."

"Be for real."

"I'm dead ass. Sex is the pinnacle of life. Hell, it *is* life—literally."

"Well, I don't mean I'm never having it again. I just mean not with him. He's completely out of the picture at this point."

"Uh-huh."

"I don't want you doing anything else. No more hook-ups with him."

"Okay," she says, twirling a loc of her hair around her finger. Whenever she does that, I know I'm in trouble.

"I'm serious."

"Right."

"Dericka!"

"What!"

"I mean it."

"No, no, I believe you."

"Good. Well, okay, I'm going to shower and go to bed."

She nods as I walk away.

"I believe you're full of shit." I hear her whisper behind my back.

"Good night, Dericka."

"Sexy dreams, Nichole."

I'm definitely going to have a lot to confess on Sunday.

CHAPTER FOUR

Gredin

THE QUIET Saturday morning I wanted to spend out on my back lawn is pierced by the squawking of my next-door neighbor's blue hyacinth macaws. I'm trying to walk off the pain from stubbing my toe on the crate of cacao I had overnighted from Hawaii and forgot I placed them by the patio door. They're the first seeds from this particular set of trees I've been cultivating and I want to be the one to taste them.

The ringing of my doorbell puts that plan on hold. The person I see on the security camera puts a sour taste in my mouth that not even a newly enhanced chocolate seed can get rid of.

She's leaning against the light pole looking up at the camera. The blue wrap-around dress she's wearing leaves nothing to the imagination. It's low-cut and tight, but she doesn't have the chest to pull it off. Unlike Nichole whose tits had me drooling in her dress.

I do have to admit she's sexy, but my dick doesn't even register her. I know he's not broken. The hard-on I got from thinking about Nichole just now proves that.

"You know better than to come here unannounced," I say, opening my door. She can't take no for an answer. If the shoe was on the other foot, I'd be charged with sexual harassment by now.

She sticks her tongue out at me as she struts by to come in. She must think it's cute, but I'm annoyed at the childish gesture.

"There's this breakfast thing going on next door that I needed a break from. The place is not the same since we lost Hef." I don't disagree. At least he kept those birds quiet. "Anyway, I'm headed to Greece tonight for a photo shoot. I just came by to give you one last chance."

"To do what?"

"I'm thinking about moving there and I want you to give me a reason to stay."

"I don't have a single one. You're not exclusive to my brand. You can model for whomever you want."

"I'm not talking about work. I'm talking about us."

"What us? There is no us."

"There could be. Think about it. We can be great to-gether. We'll be the next power couple with a cute little name combination to go along with it. We'll take over the world."

"Our names don't even go together."

"A minor technicality."

"I don't think so."

"Is having me in your bed that much of a turn-off, because that's saying something different?" She points to the bulge in my gray sweatpants.

"This has nothing to do with you," I say, tucking it back down.

"I could still help you with it. You saw what I did with that jawbreaker, right?"

"All of Los Angeles saw what you did with that jawbreaker. Which is why they sell. I appreciate it. I also appreciate the offer and as lucrative as it is, I have to decline… again."

"Are you truly turning me down?"

"I've been doing that for weeks now."

"Yeah, but I thought you were playing hard to get. I didn't think you were serious."

"Now you know I am."

"But no one ever turns me down. Look at me. Did someone make a better offer?"

"You could say that."

"Who is she? Tell me what she's offering you and I can better it. I'll even let you ass fuck me."

"Again, I don't think so."

"You're turning down fucking me in my ass. That's your thing."

"Fucking random ass isn't my thing."

"Random. So now I've been moved to the category of random?"

"Let's not make this a bigger issue than it has to be. Who I fuck has nothing to do with you."

"Who is this bitch you're fucking? What the hell does she have that I don't have?"

"My attention. Have fun in Greece."

Watching her storm away, I'm kicking myself. The mention of that jawbreaker alone should have had me hauling her ass to my bedroom. What the hell is wrong with me?

Nichole Adams is what's wrong. She's too fucking right.

"I'M COMING. I'm coming. Shit, honey."

"Yes, Bas, yes. Show me who it belongs to. Whose dick is this?"

I sit at the kitchen island, tapping my index finger on the counter top, listening to what I'm sure is a fucking encounter between my trainer, Sebastiano and my housekeeper, Rhoda, somewhere in the pantry. From the sound of things, the poor guy is getting owned by her. I hadn't realized they were getting it on and clearly, it's been happening right under my nose.

In my defense, my nose has been stuck elsewhere. Mainly up in the air, sniffing what that cute little college student that fucked my senses up when she came waltzing into my office the other day left behind in her lace panties. My dick hasn't been anywhere else since being inside her. I may have reached my personal best on abstinence. If three days can be considered abstinence. For me, it's a damn world record-breaker. I'm even turning down offers from models. Granted, I was never into her, but a win is a win.

"Rhoda, *Mio Amore*, you're killing me here," Sebastiano sucks in a breath so hard it makes *my* damn lungs hurt. The wall thuds from what sounds like him collapsing on it. I need to thicken that up. I don't want to have to hear this shit again while I'm sitting here waiting for breakfast. "You're taking all my fluids away. I need to save some for McEwen."

What the fuck did he just say?

"Why are you giving him your body fluids?"

Yeah, what she said.

"I need them for energy. You know Prince Chocolate likes to be up at six sharp for his morning workout. How am I going to keep up with him today?"

I look at the time. It's now 5:50. Good fucking luck in getting those fluids she sucked out of him back in time for that. I would cancel it for the old guy but seeing as how he just called me Prince Chocolate, I'm now in the mood to torture his ass with all ten rounds of the kickboxing match we have scheduled.

Knowing where her hands have just been, Rhoda can keep that damn spinach and mushroom omelet I had a taste for this morning. I'll pick something up later.

"Let's go," I yell to Sebastiano. I hear him scrambling around as he hushes Rhoda before the door opens and he steps out like nothing's happened.

"Why the hell are you in the pantry?" I try to keep a straight face, but it's hard not to laugh at how his hair is spiked up from where Rhoda must have been grabbing it.

"I was just looking for some water." He closes the door before I can look beyond him.

"Try the fridge next time,' I say. He goes pale when Rhoda accidentally drops something, giving herself away. I do him the favor of pretending not to hear it. "I'll meet you in the gym."

TWO HOURS later, I'm tension free and at my desk. I can think of a better stress reliever than beating the shit out of Sebastiano, but it was enough to get my mind off fucking and back on working. That is until my phone rings, distracting me.

"McEwen," I answer it.

"Hey, hey, big brother. You. Me. Tonight. Club Viper. It's ladies night. What do you say?"

"What I always say, Trip. No."

"You have zero excuses not to hang out. Your dick will thank you. *My* dick will thank you. I've been dry all week."

"It's Monday."

"Like I said, all week. My big guy needs to be dipped into something wet and tight and your club is just what I need to make it happen."

"Have fun with that."

"Come on. I need a wingman. Don't you know what month this is?"

"February. It's a phenomenon that happens once a year."

"Yeah, smart-ass, it means Valentine's Day is coming up. Single chicks are desperate to hook up and we need to take advantage. They're ripe for the plucking right now and we've got some big ass gardening shears—"

"Goodbye, Trip."

"I thought you'd see it my way. You buy the drinks and I'll bring the condoms. See you at nine."

I shake my head at myself because I'm thinking about going out with him.

Nichole

WE'VE BEEN scouring Westwood Village all weekend looking for Dericka the perfect hook-up, but so far, no luck. We thought we found one. He was a bodybuilder with tight, ripped abs who goes by the name of Biker Hoss. He had muscles so big they looked like they'd explode. He wasn't my type. He was too full of himself and his head was too small for his body, but Dericka found him hot. Too bad his brain wasn't a muscle he worked out very often because he was dumb as a damn doorknob.

Dericka, being the prodigal daughter of two neuro scientists, needs conversation with her sex. She was horny enough to overlook his low IQ but once she got his pants off, it was a wrap. Turns out those muscles weren't just from working out. His steroid use had shriveled his dick down to the size of a mini hot dog and not the ones that plump when you cook 'em.

Now, here we are on Sunset Blvd. going to ladies night at Club Viper. I showed my tits to the bouncer to sneak us in because it's some upper-crust hot spot with a cover charge we didn't want to pay. Good thing I'm blessed with a nice rack. Most times that trumps the cost of admission.

"Are you feeling it yet?" Dericka asks, holding my hand and raising it as we walk in a single file through the crowd. The place is packed. As small as it is, I'm sure it's over the maximum capacity.

"I've been feeling it since I took the first bite," I say about the weed brownies she made. "I think you put too much in. Can you OD off weed?"

"Nothing ever happens with weed. Unless you count falling asleep and overeating."

"Maybe it was a bad batch."

"I got it from Mike, so it's good shit. Just chill out. Let it do its job."

THIS TIME it's Dericka's ass and a promise to let the bouncer fuck it later that gets us into the VIP section of the club. I stay at the table we copped while she goes to the bar to get drinks.

"Nik, there's a sexy shot challenge," she says after rushing back.

"A what?"

"A sexy shot challenge. Whoever has the sexiest tequila shot wins."

"Wins what?"

"Hell if I know. But they need one more couple. And the shot's free. Let's just do it."

I drag my feet over to the bar as she pulls me behind her. The couple standing next to us is a man and a woman who look to be in their thirties. The bartender has us all stand on top of the bar so the crowd can judge our shots. The couple goes first doing a simple move where he licks the salt off her neck and downs his shot.

Oh, we so have this in the bag.

Dericka gives me a look that lets me know she knows this challenge is ours. She snatches the salt shaker from them and gives it to me while I put a lemon wedge between my teeth. The crowd goes wild when I lift my sequined silver halter top and show my rack.

"Damn, girl," some guy in the crowd yells. He follows it up with a wolf whistle.

Dericka stoops down, which is no small feat in her stilettos that make her much taller than I am even in mine. She opens her mouth just below my left boob and pours the tequila over my chest.

The harsh liquid drains off one nipple right into her mouth. When it's all gone, I sprinkle the salt and she sucks it off my nipple, running her tongue up my chest until we kiss the lemon wedge out of my mouth and into hers.

The crowd goes wild again when she takes the lemon wedge out of her mouth and holds it up in a ta-da pose. I lower my top and hold up the tequila shot the bartender gives me. I down it before taking a bow.

Gredin

I CANNOT *fucking* believe she just did that. I've been stalking her ever since I spotted her coming into the club. When I approved this stupid tequila challenge I did it while being distracted by her. I didn't even know what I was agreeing to, but thank fuck I approved it. The damn thing was worth seeing her in action.

Nichole Adams is by far the sluttiest, kinkiest virgin I've ever had the pleasure of fucking. She's actually the *only* virgin I've ever had the pleasure of fucking and I enjoyed every minute of that damn tease she and that friend of hers just gave. That *has* to be the roommate.

"I think we've just found our sluts for tonight, bro," Trip says, clearly as turned on by the tequila tease as I am. Although, I already guessed that by him yelling at Nichole when she showed her tits.

"Trip…" I hate when he comes here picking over the girls like lambs going off to slaughter. I want to tell him to go fuck himself, as I often do, but this time I agree with him.

"Finally, your ass is in the game," he says.

"What the hell are you talking about?"

"You're down for tonight's fuckathon. Unless that boner in your pants is for me. And if it is, I hate to break it to you, dude, but you're not my type. I like girls. Preferably with pussies. No, *definitely* with pussies. Pussies are a must-have."

"Shut the fuck up, Trip."

I adjust my pants, tucking down my painfully engorged cock. I see Nichole walking toward her table. I get up to go after her.

"Okay, we've got a game plan," Trip says, catching on quickly and getting up to come with me. "You work on her and I'll do the same with her hot-ass girlfriend. Let's just hope they're not exclusive and that they're into guys because bi-chicks give the best head. Am I right?"

I don't answer. I've already tuned him out before he can say the last word. All my focus is on Nichole. I can't take my eyes off her. I'm like a heat-seeking missile honed in on only one target. I'm mesmerized by the sway of her hips as she walks. More like a dog in heat as she puts it, and I can't wait to be stuck together with her ass.

Nichole

"TOLD YOU we had this," Dericka says. We're walking back to our table with our newly won bottle of *Patron Silver.*

"Yeah, well for all the good it did me. My boobs are on fire. I'm going to wash this tequila off me."

"Hurry back. I'm ready to break this sucker open," she says, holding up the tequila bottle.

"Yeah, yeah, keep your shirt on."

"Look who's talking."

I give her the finger, then go in search of the bathroom.

Of course, the line is out the door. And wouldn't you know, I have a sudden urge to pee just looking at it.

I lean forward, counting the girls in front of me and thinking up ways to bum ahead a few spaces when someone grabs me from behind and spins me around. Before I can even think of how to respond, lips come crashing into mine and hands are groping me. I relax into him, knowing instinctively who it is. I don't even have to look at him. The way his body feels against mine is proof enough. I wrap my arms around his shoulders and tangle my fingers in the hair at the nape of his neck.

"Mmm," he moans into my mouth when I allow him to stick his tongue inside.

His arms circle my waist. He lifts me and spins me around again, backing me into a dark corner away from prying eyes.

"Gredin," I moan his name at the feel of his hand at the hem of my skirt, going underneath it to cup my ass. I gasp when he brushes my panties aside and slips a finger in me.

"Fuck," he groans at the gush of wetness. "My little virgin is horny."

"Shit," I breathe at the feel of him fucking me with his finger. I can't help but grind into his hand.

"You on that bar. That shit was hot. I need to see these tits." His hand creeps up my shirt, exposing me. I arch my back into his mouth as he sucks my nipples, tasting the tequila and salt. "Mmm, so good. I want to get drunk off these."

"Hey." I push him away, looking around to make sure no one sees us.

"I want you," he says, trying to turn my head back so he can kiss me. "I can't fucking get you off my mind."

"We agreed to one time only. A fuck-and-done." I don't know if I'm trying to remind him or myself.

"Let's make it two fucks."

"What kind of a girl do you take me for?" I'm trying not to laugh at the statement and the look he gives when it hits his ears.

"I'm sorry." He's still undeterred from groping me. "I

could have sworn that was *you* with that girl attached to your tit on top of the bar a moment ago."

"Yeah, well these tits belong to her tonight," I say, shaking my rack in his face for a good-natured tease before swatting his hands off me and walking away.

"We'll have to see about that," he says to my retreating back.

I get back in the line that's grown considerably longer, banging my head against the wall I'm leaning on.

Stupid. Stupid. Stupid.

Why did I just walk away from him?

"You're going to kill yourself if you keep doing that," the girl in front of me says.

"So what?"

The dampness between my legs that Gredin just caused is making me uncomfortable, and the fact that I'm now horny and I just told my release to get lost is making me irritable.

"Drunk bitch," she says under her breath. Dericka would get a kick out of me actually giving someone a reason to call me a bitch.

I give up on this whole bathroom thing and go back to her.

"Wow, you know how to hurry," she says to me when I sit down.

"I saw Gredin."

"Did you just have a quickie? I mean, but damn, that was *really* quick, though. Where is he now?"

"I didn't have a quickie. I blew him off."

"You didn't. Why the hell would you do that?"

"I don't freaking know. God, I'm still *high*. I panicked or something," I say and she has the nerve to laugh. "What's so funny?"

"You are *soooo* into him."

"Bullshit."

"Okay, whatever. Forget him. I have something better for us tonight."

"What is it?"

"Well, the owner of this here fine establishment saw our little slut show on the bar and wants to meet you."

"Me? Why me? Why not you?"

"Because I'm kinda into his brother. While you were busy avoiding your crush, I was over here being felt up by the finest, sexiest piece of muscle meat I've ever seen. He's older. A white guy. Probably in his thirties so score one for me."

"Good. Now we can finally stop looking."

"You know it. I've got this in the bag."

"I still don't know what all this has to do with me."

"Like I said, he's here with his brother—his *older* brother, by the way, since you're into that now. He's the one that owns the place and they're both waiting for us upstairs."

"There's an upstairs?" I look up at the ceiling.

"Private party time, boo boo."

"Oh, no it's not. No way in all hell am I going up there for some hoe shit," I say, folding my arms over my chest and cringing at the sting that's still on my irritated nipples.

CHAPTER FIVE

Nichole

THEY NEED to turn the air on in here. It's too hot. Or maybe it's just from the tequila I've been drinking. Either way, I feel like I'm about to pass out.

"Ouch." I snatch my boob out of Dericka's mouth. "You're supposed to be sucking the tequila off, not biting my goddamn nipple."

"It tastes good and I'm hungry."

"Cannibal," I grumble, pulling my top down. "I think you drew blood."

"Vampire," she corrects me.

"Shut up."

We're being watched by a muscle brain with bazookas for arms and his gangly friend. I roll my eyes when they come over to talk to us.

"Hey, hey, hey, foxy ladies. What is goin' on?" The large, overly orange tanned one says. He goes so far as to flex his bicep. I down a tequila shot to stop from laughing, but Dericka is not so kind.

"Oh, *hell* no," she says to him before grabbing my hand and pulling me from our table.

"Where are we going?"

"Upstairs. I'm getting laid tonight and it sure as hell isn't going to be by steroid boy and his faithful sidekick back there."

"Okay, but I'm just watching. You can count me out of any action."

"Right. Whatever your little horny ass says."

"I mean it, Dericka. Just because I fucked a guy once doesn't make me a fucking person."

"Oh, yeah. No, I hear what you're saying. Nichole Adams is *not* a fucking person."

"Exactly."

"Maybe you can be a fucking hybrid."

"What?"

"You know. Kinda like in transition."

"I'm way too drunk and high for this conversation," I say when we hit the stairs. "Is there no elevator?"

"It's only around twenty steps."

"I'm sure the handicap association wouldn't see it that way."

"Boy, you're just a ball of fun tonight."

"What do you expect? I just blew off Gredin and now I have to watch while *you* get some."

"That's what besties are for." She grins.

As she knocks on the door, I look down both ends of the hallway for possible escape routes, just in case some nut-job is waiting for us on the other side. I jump like an idiot when the door opens.

"Hey, sexy," a gorgeous guy says. He's all smiles at Dericka.

He's hot. He has blue eyes, sandy blonde hair that's naturally wavy, and skin that's been kissed by the sun. I bet he surfs or maybe he plays volleyball or whatever the hell beach guys do. He's built, but not too much. He's the type that can easily pick you up and fuck you around the room, but not the type that will slam you down like a thousand-pound dumbbell while yelling at the top of his lungs in some stupid weightlifting competition. He's *so* Dericka's type.

"Hi, yourself," she says. Her voice is all airy, a dead giveaway that she's into him. There's no way I'm pulling her out of here. "This is my best friend, Nichole."

"Hey, pretty Nikki." He flashes me a smile.

"Hi," I say, almost giddy at the compliment. *Oh, he's good.*

"Come on in," he says to me while pulling Dericka in for a kiss.

I roll my eyes at them already getting carried away, pawing each other at the door as I walk past them. I wonder if there's a TV or something I can watch. Listening to Dericka already moaning, I might just end up playing with my damn self. It's already making me horny.

"Whoa," I say when I'm pressed up against a wall.

Familiar lips find mine and I moan into them even louder than Dericka. Determined fingers trace their way up my top to my boobs, making me hiss at the rough contact.

"Tell me again who these belong to tonight, *pretty Nikki*?"

"Wha— what are you doing up here, Gredin?"

"He's my brother." He cocks his head towards the door where Dericka and tall hot blonde guy are still going at it.

"He looks nothing like you."

"He's my brother from a different mother. By marriage."

"Oh… um." I try to think, but his lips are nibbling up my neck.

"You taste so fucking good. So sweet and salty."

"I'm supposed to not be doing anything," I moan in a weak protest.

I cut my eyes to see if Dericka can help bail me out but she's already left the door and is now buck booty ass naked riding tall hot blonde guy on the couch.

Fucking Dericka, I swear the girl has no shame.

"You won't have to do a damn thing, baby." *Baby?* He spins me around so that I'm facing the wall. I feel him inch up my skirt, flinging it up over my ass. I yelp when his hand lands hard on my cheek, smacking it. "Who does this belong to?"

"I… uh. Oh, my God," I moan when his long middle finger slips inside me. "Mmm."

"And this?" he asks of my dripping wet pussy. "Who does this belong to?" His mouth is at my ear, tickling it with his warm breath while we grind together with him finger fucking me. "Answer me." His voice is low and needy. My pussy clamps around his finger making him growl with my earlobe caught in his teeth.

"You," I answer. "It's you. It's you. It's you."

"Damn right it's me."

I whimper in protest when he removes his finger to rip open a condom and put it on. He enters me so good that my moan comes out too loud and sharp from the back of my throat.

"Jesus, bro, you're killing it over there," his tall hot blonde brother says.

I hear Dericka laugh. I try to cover my mouth to shut myself up as Gredin fucks me. My face is now flaming hot from embarrassment. I cannot believe my second shot at real dick is in front of Dericka and her fuck buddy. Gredin's brother, no less. I'm such a slut.

"Let them hear you," Gredin says, uncovering my mouth.

"Gredin, I don't…" I stop and look over at our audience.

Dericka is still straddling tall hot blonde guy, looking at me over her shoulder while he is doing the same.

"You're fucking beautiful. So hot and sexy. Let them see. What happens here tonight will never leave this room."

My body relaxes back into him as he fucks me from behind again.

HE PULLS out and turns me around, stopping long enough to take off his shirt. His hands go up my skirt again, taking off my sopping wet panties. I watch as he brings them to his nose, inhaling them before stuffing them in his pocket and stepping out of his pants.

He helps me out of my skirt, taking my heels with it, before moving up to my top.

I hiss again when the fabric touches my raw nipples. His eyes darken at the sight of them before he leaves me. I stand naked biting my lip as I glance in Dericka and tall hot blonde guy's direction, but they're too busy fucking again to notice me.

Gredin returns, twisting open a bottle of water as he stalks toward me naked. My eyes can't help but glue themselves to his dick that's in full salute as he walks. I sigh in relieved pleasure as he empties the bottle all over my chest. The cool water instantly soothes my nipples and cleanses them of the salt and tequila.

He takes one in his mouth and gently suckles it.

"Oh, my God, that feels so good," I whisper. My hands are knotted in his hair as his tongue makes a hot wet line to my other nipple, giving it some much-needed attention.

"You are a thirst quencher, baby. But I've gotten nowhere near my fill of you yet."

His dick presses against my pubic fuzz. *Shit, I knew I should have shaved this morning.*

He lifts my leg, hooking it around his forearm to open me up. My breath hitches when he slides into me. My pussy stretches to accommodate his dick in this new position like it did the first time he fucked me. And like the first time, he is wanting to be gentle.

"Fuck me," I say, reminding him of my enjoyment of the fucking he gave in his office.

"Fuck," he hisses.

My arms wrap around him to keep my balance as he pounds hard into me. I feel every inch of him as he pulls out, only to delve right back in harder and deeper. He is hitting me so deep he's nearly lifting me off the ground. I have to stand on my tiptoes.

My body starts to tingle with sensations shooting out of every nerve coming together deliciously between my legs. The puddle that his dick has been fucking is now a flood dribbling down my thigh. I'm so close.

My standing leg goes weak, so he lifts me. Instantly, I drag my much-too-heavy legs up, wrapping them around his waist. He pounds into me hard and deep as I bounce on his dick in rhythm with him.

"That's right. Come for me, pretty Nikki."

"Oh, God," I moan out loud. My second orgasm at his hands hits me without warning, making my whole body shake in sheer pleasure.

"Aw, fuck," he says, coming with me.

My nails dig into his shoulders. It's that good. I convulse as he pounds into me, unrelenting until every ounce of strength is drained from me.

"No more. No more. No more."

"Fuck, you are drowning me, baby," he says. His voice is tinged with a sexual need. It turns me on, but I still laugh at his words, burying my head in his neck. He growls at the sound.

We sit on the couch next to tall hot blonde guy while Dericka rides him. By the smell of her, she's had her share of orgasms already. The roots of her twists are shiny with sweat and what looks like a little cum plastered to her forehead. I'm not faring much better. I can feel the ends of my hair sticking to my back. I had gone to the trouble of straightening it earlier, but now as wet as it is, it's curling right back up.

I brush her hair off her shoulder. She takes it as a come-on and pulls me into her for a kiss. I go with it. Kissing her is like breathing to me now.

"Fuck yeah," tall hot blonde guy says. He sounds completely turned on by us making out while being fucked by him and his brother.

Gredin's dick gets hard again inside me as he watches me make out with her. He starts to pound me again.

"Oh, God, yes," I break the kiss long enough to moan before tonguing Dericka again.

Her mouth tastes like what I'm guessing is tall hot blonde guy and I wonder what part of him I'm tasting.

Gredin hits me at just the right spot and I come again, moaning in Dericka's mouth.

I don't know how it happens. I'm too far in a sex-induced haze but somehow, I end up being pulled off Gredin's dick. I watch as my cum drips out of me all over his legs. Now, I'm flat on my back on the chaise part of the couch.

Gredin pulls off his condom and slides his dick in my mouth. Dericka is between my legs eating my pussy. I grind into her tongue as she licks and twirls my clit up into a tight frenzied coil. It's seconds from exploding and I move faster, working towards it. She's finger-fucking me as best she can with her tall hot blonde fucking her from behind.

I grab hold of the base of Gredin and cup his balls while I suck his cum off his tip.

"Shit," he moans as I take him in as best I can. His hips move back and forth, fucking my mouth.

Dericka brings me to orgasm and it comes out in a muffled cry with dick still stuffed in my mouth. I writhe on the couch, riding my third wave in less than an hour.

"You want to taste it, baby?" Gredin asks. My only answer is to suck him harder. "Open your mouth."

He pulls out and I do as I'm told, opening my mouth wide with my tongue sticking out. He pumps his dick twice, grunting as hot milky white cum shoots from his dick down my throat. My lips curl around his tip to suck the rest.

I lay like a starfish on the chaise lounge. I'm spent, unable to move. I've never come so much at the hands of multiple people all at once, or all of *never*. Dericka must have come too because she's keeled over on the couch.

Now I'm in her tall hot blonde guy's line of sight. His dick is still just as hard as Gredin's but not nearly as big. My eyes bulge at how full his condom is as he moves toward me. He must notice because he grins at me with his dick in his hand, stroking it.

"You want to try some of this, Nikki?" he asks me.

I find my legs and use them to scoot away from him. I almost topple off the chaise before Gredin grabs me. I wrap myself around him. His lips laugh on mine as he kisses me.

"Hey," Dericka yells at her tall hot blonde guy, smacking him on his bare ass. "She's not a fucking person."

"What?" he says, looking completely confused. "What the hell is she?"

"She's a virgin, okay."

"A virgin," he says, yanking his head back toward me kissing Gredin. "The way she's going at it with him?"

He forgets all about it when Dericka takes off his condom and starts sucking him off. His moans are making me horny again.

I feel Gredin's dick at my groin. I reach down and feel how slick it is with a new condom on so I put it inside me.

"Mmm," is all he says before my lips find him again.

I ride him like it's going out of style. Rising to his tip, I sit down, plunging him back into me again and again, working him over with my grinding hips. He grabs the ends of my hair and pulls my head back, exposing my neck. His teeth sink into the soft skin as he orgasms, filling his condom up with cum.

"Fuck, Nikki. Shit."

His moans are my undoing and I come again, holding on to him as I think I may just lose my mind from the strength of it. His fingers dig into my hips as we both grind out the last of our orgasms.

"Fuck, blondie," tall hot blonde guy yells at Dericka, who he's now banging wildly on the couch. Her hands scratch down his back, leaving trickles of blood in their wake as she comes. Her heels are at his ass pushing him in deeper. Her purple-painted toes are curled tight.

Damn, she looks hot when she comes. I rest my forehead on Gredin's, trying to get control of my breathing. If this is what clubbing and hooking up are all about, I'll be doing it more often.

"I CAN'T believe I just fucked you in front of your brother," I tell Gredin, as he leads me into a bathroom. My tequila/ bud brownie high must be fading as I realize what I just did. "My second fuck in life and it was a twosome that turned into a threesome which was nearly a foursome.

"Shit like that happens," he says.

"Do you guys do this a lot?"

He shakes his head.

"First time I agreed."

"Well, I don't feel too slutty since I was your first."

"I'm the only man you've ever fucked. That, by definition, says you're not slutty."

I laugh at the truth of the statement.

"I'm surprised this office has this big of a bathroom," I say as we step into the shower together.

"It has two," he says, sponging me down with soap that smells like sandalwood and magnolia.

I can see myself snuggling up to him if he smelled like this. I banish the thought, remembering our one-and-done rule.

"The other one is as big as this?"

"Just about. I prefer a lot of space, except for certain things. I prefer them tight."

I catch my breath when his finger brushes my clit.

"Well, it looks like you found it," I say.

"Mmm, I sure did."

"I meant the big space," I laugh, turning toward the shower head to wash off, being careful not to get all of my hair wet.

"You have a great ass." I look over my shoulder to see him examining it. "My dick would fit perfectly inside. I want to claim it."

"What happened to two and done?"

"For this ass, I'll agree to three and done."

"Not with my asshole you won't. I have to shit out of that, you know. How well would it work with you sticking your dick up in there? And that's just gross." He laughs, smacking my ass as I step out of the shower to grab a towel. "Your brother seems nice."

"My brother's a jerk."

"You lie. I can tell you get along with him."

"Fine, he's nice. But not nice enough for you to fuck, I noted."

"Hey, what can I say? I'm a one-dick chick." I shrug.

"Is that so?"

"Yes, it is. Well, for now anyway."

He raises an angry eyebrow at me as I shrug a little again and leave the room.

The fact that I feel embarrassed being in a towel in front of people who just saw me naked is saying a lot. I still hurry to find my things so I can get dressed.

I find my left heel right away and put it on. Walking with one shoe on and one off, I go picking up my clothes that are strewn about the room. Dericka comes out of the other bathroom and starts doing the same.

"Ow," I say when we both bend down too close to each other and bump heads.

"Sorry," she laughs, rubbing the top of her head.

"Damn, they're fucking hot," tall hot blonde guy says as he and Gredin watch the show we didn't even know we were putting on.

"What's your name, anyway?" I ask him, bouncing up and down for balance while putting on my other heel.

"Trip." He grins. "This guy's baby brother." He points his thumb at Gredin.

"By another mother," I say.

"Right."

He pulls a fully dressed Dericka to him for a final goodbye kiss.

Their moaning gets me going again, but Gredin still has that damn angry eyebrow raised at me. I don't know what has crawled up his ass and died. I clear my throat, trying not to squirm under his glare. I can almost see the steam coming from him.

"Let's go, Dericka." I'm practically dragging her to the door.

"Girl, will you wait a damn minute," she says, almost losing her balance, but I don't listen. "Okay, okay," she says, wobbling behind me. "What's the hurry?"

"I need to find some lotion before my skin starts to itch."

Gredin

"FUCK, BRO. That shit was hot," Trip says, moving his back around to ease the pain of his love marks. I move my shoulders, doing the same. "Nichole was all over you. I don't for a minute believe that virgin act she had going on."

I shake my head.

"She was a virgin before I fucked her. And keep your big mouth shut about this. I promised her it would never leave this room."

"What the hell am I going to say and who would I say it to? Besides, I thought virgins bled." He looks around the white leather couch for evidence. He only finds cum, which I text my manager to have a crew come over and clean.

"I fucked her in my office the other day. She's one of the Alpha Psi I donated the Rolex to."

"Wait, wait, wait, so you knew who she was? And you fucked her in your office just like that."

"I was doing her a favor."

"A favor. You are one lucky son of a bitch."

"Not for long. She's planning on fucking someone else."

"Well, yeah," he says and I glare at him. "I mean, right?"

"I own her virginity."

"What the hell does that mean, Gredin? She has to take a vow of celibacy now just because you fucked her first. Hold on, are you planning on seeing her again?" I just stare at him. "Man, I can't take you *anywhere*." He throws his head back. "This was just a fun night. A hook-up, bro. Damn. Who the fuck looks for serious shit in a club?"

"I don't want serious. I haven't gotten enough of her yet. Until I do, I don't want anyone else fucking her. And don't act like you wouldn't do Dericka again."

"Shit yeah, I'd do that little hell cat again. My back is on fire from her claws. Swear to God, my balls nearly collapsed from that last orgasm she gave me."

"TMI, Trip. TM *fucking* I."

CHAPTER SIX

Nichole

I SIDE-EYE DERICKA as she sighs for the third time in less than five minutes. We're in my bed watching *Think Like a Man*. The munchies from the weed have kicked in and we're binging on Oreo cookies, potato chips, and wine. We've been home for over two hours and she's still going on and on about Trip.

"Who names their kid Trip?" I ask her.

"It's short for Tripper."

"Like that's any better."

"To hear him tell it, his mom liked some guy on a sitcom from the eighties."

"Okay, cute."

"He is."

"I can't believe you let him come in your hair," I say watching her wrap it up in her headscarf now that it's been washed and dried. She already made an appointment to get her twists redone.

"I didn't *let* him. He just had bad aim. But damn he was good."

"Will you let it go already," I say when she sighs again.

"I can't help it and don't act like you're not over there wishing it was Gredin in here with you instead of me."

"Not true. I stand firmly by the hoes-before-bros rule and besides, he and I are going nowhere. I'll probably never see him again. And you won't see Trip again either."

"Hey, speak for yourself, okay. Don't drag me and my need to get laid into it."

"You're already in it. We need to keep them in their lanes. Just accept them as the marks in our bedposts that they are."

"Are you finished? Because I didn't buy a word of that little lecture."

"It's true."

"Right. Tell that to the box of his chocolates I saw you stash in your shopping cart."

"You're such a bitch."

"And you love it. Now break out the chocolates."

"Fine," I say, opening my bedside drawer and taking out the little red box of Valentine's Day chocolates.

"Oh, my God," Dericka says, biting into one, wiping the caramel that came out in a long strand and fell on her chin.

I do the same, picking one that looks like it has nuts in it. Jackpot. It's filled with almonds. My absolute favorite.

"Mmm," I moan. "I can see how he's made a fortune selling this."

"We need to get more," Dericka says.

"Definitely. We're going to be huge by the time Valentine's Day comes. We won't be able to fit through the door."

"And it will be so worth it," she says, picking up another chocolate.

"Definitely," I say, biting into another one. "Mmm."

I DON'T know what time we finally fell asleep, but the annoying sound of my alarm clock says it wasn't long enough.

"I feel like shit." I hear Dericka mumble next to me with her head under the pillow to drown out the sound.

"Remind me of this feeling the next time you convince me to go out on a school night," I tell her.

"Whoever made it so college kids had to go to class was an idiot."

"Tell me about it," I say, getting up to go to the bathroom.

"Don't spend all morning in there."

"I'm not even in there yet," I say, slipping on my house shoes. "And don't even think about taking that last chocolate," I threaten her when I hear the box being opened.

"Damn."

I skip the shower since I took one last night and settle on brushing my teeth. Try as I might, I can't stop thinking about Gredin. I still want to know what had him so pissed off last night. As far as I could tell, he had a great time. I shake my head as I spit out the toothpaste. Why do I even care about his moody ass and what pissed him off? Anyway, it couldn't have been something I did. Or could it?

This is just great. I can't seem to follow my own advice and forget about him. I don't know what's wrong with me. I should have left it at the one-and-done.

"Did you fall in?" Dericka yells at me.

"Shut up," I say before rinsing my mouth out and leaving the bathroom. She's right where I left her. The bitch has no intentions of getting up anytime soon. "Now that operation get Dericka laid is over, what are we going to do?" I sit back down on the bed, in no hurry either. "We still don't have anything good going on for V-day?"

"It's too early to panic. We still have time to make something happen."

"If you say so. Just let me know when it *is* time to panic."

I SIT down with a heavy thud at the table in the far corner of the library. This is the only place I can avoid Dericka and her constant talking about Trip. She's so dickmatized she doesn't know what to do with herself. Big Bird couldn't even get her attention today.

Just when I thought I was going to get some work done, in walks trouble. I thought I dodged him at the basketball courts. Clearly, he saw me because here he is, wiping the sweat off his face with his T-shirt.

"I thought that was you I saw coming in here."

"Guilty," I say. "How're you doing, Terrence?"

"Better now that I'm with you." He sits down too close to me. He's been playing hard and is in desperate need of a shower. "Damn, you look good." He leans back to check me out.

"Yeah, thanks. But listen, I really need to get these sketches done before my art class." I hold up my sketch pad to emphasize the point.

"It's all good. I wanted to know if you changed your mind about Valentine's Day. I still have the tickets to that concert. It's going to be lit."

"I bet." I'm actually thinking about it. We can go as friends.

"You can spend the night at my place. My roommate is staying with his girl—"

Nope. Nevermind.

"I don't think so."

"You sure? We can go for round two."

"We didn't even have a round one, Terrence."

"I was getting that first nut out the way."

"Right. It's okay. Like you said, it's all good."

"Don't be like that. You know I'm into you. Especially when you come in here looking like this. You always got to tease me."

"I don't base my outfits on you. It's not that deep."

"Oh, it's like that?"

"Look, so we're clear. I just want to be friends."

"When did you turn into a bitch?"

"Okay, you know what," I say getting my shit so I can leave. "I'm just going to call it a day. Have the one you deserve."

Ugh, he's right. I was being a bitch for no reason. All the poor guy did was come into his hands. I don't know why I treated him that way, but the thought of having sex with him pissed me off for some reason. I know I shouldn't compare him to Gredin but I can't help it. What the hell is wrong with me?

I call Dericka while I walk through the parking lot.

"I'm done for the day. I was a bitch to Terrence and it just killed my mood."

"Good, you *should* be a bitch to that asshole. What did he do?"

"Just showed me once again why college boys suck. They give nothing but low vibrations."

"You got that right and I beat you to it, by the way. I'm already home."

"I figured. You want anything from the Coffee Hut?"

"Iced coffee and a sesame seed bagel."

"Okay. I'll see you in twenty."

I hop in my car, toss my stuff in the passenger seat, and plug my phone into the car charger. Before I can even set it down it rings again. I shake my head thinking it's Dericka wanting something else. It's not her but I smile all the same when I see who it really is.

"Hi, Grandma."

"And why haven't you called me?"

"Because I'm a horrible granddaughter."

"No. Not my grandbaby," she says and I grin. "Are you on your way to class?"

"I'm all done for the day. I was just going to get something decadent to eat."

"That's the reason I'm calling. I put four of my cakes in the oven a while ago."

"You're taking orders already?" She usually doesn't start baking until Easter.

"Folks are requesting them early this year. A man from Montgomery placed this order for his wife. Said people are talking about my cakes from all around."

"And they should. Everyone knows Pearline Adams makes the best cakes in the entire south."

"Tell the truth and shame the devil. Anyway, it made me think of you. Do you still need my chocolate cake recipe?"

"I do," I say, looking in my bag for a pen, wondering what the hell I did with it. "I don't have anything to write it down with right now, but I want to make it for Dericka on Valentine's Day."

"Is that what you all are doing?"

"We have no lives or dates."

"There has to be somebody."

"Nope. Guys suck. They don't make them like Grandpa anymore."

"Well, baby, they didn't make *him*. The way he is is all thanks to me. I had to undo what his mother did to him. And don't you ever tell him I said that."

"I won't," I laugh.

"What happened to that nice boy you were seeing? What was his name?"

"Terrence?" I say with a roll of my eyes. "Forget him."

"Aw, that's a shame. I liked him."

"There aren't many people you don't like."

"Now that's not true. I didn't care for that one boy you had in the sixth grade. The one that kept pulling your hair."

"What boy?"

"You know the one. He's Bessie's grandboy. Used to run around with his shoes on the wrong feet."

"Monte," I squeal. "I can't believe you still remember that."

"Bless his little heart," she says, making me laugh. "Baby, I have to go. I smell my cakes. I'll email you the recipe."

"Since when do you email?"

"Since cousin Lionel taught me."

"Cousin Lionel? Last time I saw him, he couldn't even work his cell phone."

"He had the nerve to take a class about all the latest technology down at the senior center. Now, he won't shut up about how we all need to have debit cards."

"He's right."

"I'll tell you like I told him and that little girl down at the gas company who wants me to pay online; my checkbook works just fine."

"Whatever you say."

"Love you, baby, and don't go so long without calling me. You hear?"

"I won't. Love you and give my love to Grandpa."

I toss my phone in the console to let it keep charging before I pull my visor down to check myself out.

My mocha-colored lipstick has worn off so I run a finger over my lips, trying to fix what's left of it. My eyebrows furrow when I feel the zit that's forming on my forehead, a sure sign that my period is about to start. I slap the visor closed and pull out of the parking lot, heading toward San Vicente. I can already taste the large hazelnut frappe and peach cobbler donut I'm going to get.

CHAPTER SEVEN

Gredin

PULL INTO work feeling like trampled-on shit. I need a fucking orgasm. Correction: I need *Pretty Nikki* to give me a fucking orgasm. The question is how do I make that happen without looking like the desperate sack of shit that I am? Even Trip with his whoring ass can't think of a way to make me look good while begging to be fucked by a virgin.

Fuck my life.

I enter the lobby and the smell of candy hits me. It spritzes out of the air fresheners that are strategically placed throughout the building. Normally, I like the smell, but right now it reminds me of the sweet scent of Nikki's enchanted pussy. I punch the elevator button a little too hard, thoroughly disgusted with myself.

Nodding to my assistant, and taking the coffee she offers, I head straight to my office. No sooner do I sit down than my head connoisseur, Francisco walks in.

"The taste test results are in," he says.

"Let's hear it."

"Maybe you should drink some of that coffee first."

"Just give me the damn results."

"They hate it."

"Still?" I turn on my computer and cue up the video of the taste test from this morning. "They're spitting it out."

"I don't know what to tell you," he says.

"What the fuck do you mean you don't know what to tell me? This cake is set to launch in a few days so you'd better tell me something. It's going worldwide and the people we hired to taste it are spitting it out. What are they saying?"

"Some are saying it's dry while the rest are saying it's bitter."

"But the last group said it was too wet and sweet."

"I don't know what to tell you." He throws his hands up.

"You better think of something and fast. Do you know how far in the hole we're going to be if this cake fails?"

"I know. I got my best guys working on it."

"Work harder. Tweak the recipe again and have the same people taste it. I want results by the end of today."

"I'm on it," he says, rushing out.

Shit!

IT'S FIVE in the afternoon and I'm still tasting chocolate cake. The tasters are right. This shit is disgusting. This cake was supposed to launch as the flagship of our new company. I don't know what possessed me to branch out into desserts. Our candy is doing fine, phenomenal in fact. This month is projected to give us our biggest profits to date. This cake debacle could ruin it.

When my grandfather retired and left me his company, I swore I'd make him proud. Now, I just might let him down. The threat of that is devastating to me.

I slide the last piece of cake closer so I can taste it, but just the smell of it is making me gag. It has our signature chocolate which I love, but I can tell it's dry. I don't even have to taste it to know it's bad. I toss it in the trashcan with the other thirty I've already tried.

Running out of patience and time, I call it a day. I need to take a step back and refocus. I make the thirty-minute drive home with no change in my foul mood.

Walking through my front door, I shrug out of my coat and toss it on the couch along with my tie and Rolex before going over to the bar to pour myself a drink. Hearing Rhoda coming up behind me, I turn to give her my attention.

"Would you like me to make you something to eat before I go?"

"No thanks. I'm full off too much chocolate cake."

"I can't wait to taste it." Her strawberry blonde hair is down from its bun, the way she always has it right before she leaves. She's dressed a little sexier than normal though. I'm guessing she's about to meet up with Sebastiano.

"The recipe isn't quite right," I tell her.

"I'm sure you'll figure it out. I remember you had a similar issue with your heart-shaped suckers a few years ago, and look how well they're doing. They're like the *Peeps* of Valentine's Day. Your cake will be the same."

"From your mouth," I say. "Do you happen to know anything about baking cakes, Rhoda?"

"No, I'm afraid not. My mom was the confectioner in our family. I never picked it up."

"That's a shame."

"Try not to worry. These things have a way of working out."

"I'm sure you're right."

"Good night, Mr. McEwen."

"Drive safely."

I pour another drink and take it into my bedroom to change. I may as well get a workout in.

"Not so fast, bro." Trip walks in with a large pizza in one hand and a case of beer in the other. I should have set the damn alarm when Rhoda left.

"What are you doing here?"

"What does it look like?" He sets the pizza and beer down on the coffee table. "I'm about to inhale this and you're going to help me."

I don't even bother arguing with him. I'd just be wasting my breath so I sit down as he pops open two of the beers. He finds a movie and I find myself enjoying it before the doorbell rings. I'm about to take out my phone to see the door cam but he stops me.

"I already know what it is." He gets up to get it. I don't even question him because I'm genuinely curious as to who the hell he has coming to my door. "I had Mom courier it over," he says of the large white box he's carrying.

"Shit." I grimace when I see what it is. Just the sight of it makes me want to vomit.

"I know. I know. You have a version coming out, but listen, you need to try this thing." He disappears into the kitchen and comes back out with a knife, forks, and two plates. "It's the best thing you'll ever put in your mouth."

"Do you know how much cake I had to taste today?"

"Just give it a try." He cuts a piece and plops it on my plate. "It will be the last one you'll ever want to eat. Trust me."

"I'll pass."

"I'm not leaving until you try it and you know I mean it."

With a roll of my eyes and a churn of my stomach, I hastily grab a fork and shove some into my mouth.

"Jesus," I whisper, getting a taste of it.

"What did I tell you."

"This is amazing. It's everything I want in a cake: buttery, moist, chocolaty, and melts in your mouth." I take another bite trying to figure out what the hell is in it because, fuck me, it's good.

"Told you."

"Where the hell did your mom get it?" I ask, looking at the box, but no name is on it.

"Dad had it shipped out from Alabama for her. There's a lady there that makes them right out of her own kitchen."

"Her own kitchen. You've got to be shitting me. She doesn't have a bakery?"

"Nope. Just her little old self and an oven according to Dad."

"How'd he find out about her from all the way down in Alabama?"

"You know Dad. If it's something that tastes good, he's going to find it. You need to have her cakes in your new company."

No truer words had ever been spoken, especially by my brother.

"As much as it pains me to admit it, you're right. I need to find this woman."

"Well, don't bug Mom about it right now. She's having a date night with Dad. The only reason she agreed to send me the cake was to get me out of her hair."

"Date night. They're the only two fucking people in the house."

"I guess it takes more than rubbing two sticks together to keep the sparks flying."

"As far as I'm concerned, our parents have no sparks. They're too old. They need to cut that shit out before one of them has a heart attack."

"Exactly. Why do you think I'm over here being a nuisance to you and not bugging them? Mom gave me that cake to block my cock block."

"How did you know I was home anyway?"

"GPS."

Our parents had us download an app so we could track each other on our phones a few years ago. I did it out of courtesy to them, but my bonehead brother is actually using the damn thing.

"I can't believe you're tracking my ass with that shit."

"Believe it. Somebody has to keep tabs on you. Enough talk about cakes and my stalking tendencies."

I take that to mean he's leaving. I'm sick of talking to his ass anyway.

"Fine with me."

"I came up with a plan to get your girl."

That piques my interest.

"I'm listening. At this point, I'll try anything. Even if it comes from you."

"Your confidence in me is touching."

"Are you going to tell me?"

"Well, now I don't know."

"Spit it out."

"Okay, okay, keep your shirt on. I'll tell you. I think I need to make a special donation to the Alpha Psi in the girls' names."

"Hey, anything for charity."

Nichole

"NOT MUCH going on down there, is it?" Dericka tilts her head to one side and then the other as she stares at the naked white-stoned statue of some ancient god.

We're at the Getty Villa Museum in Pacific Palisades, one of my favorite places. The first time I came here I spent hours taking it all in. I'd heard of the place, but I had no idea it was like this. It took my breath away and it still does. I dragged Dericka here so she could keep me company while I sketch the statue for art class, and she's right. There's not much going on down there.

"True. He's not very well endowed," I say to her. He's also too skinny. Gredin has more muscle to grab onto. He's also chiseled to perfection. Just thinking about his body has me on the verge of overheating. He'd put these statues to shame. They definitely broke the mold when they made him. "Maybe the sculptor was being modest."

"Humph." She stomps away. Her hands are deep in her pants pockets since a security guard yelled at her for touching a painting.

I find her in the garden looking at her phone.

"What's up?" I ask her when she rolls her eyes.

"Cierra is calling a house meeting later today."

"Oh, God," I groan. "What is it now?"

"Didn't say, but we're 'required' to be there. Somebody probably forgot to make their bed again."

I take out my phone and sure enough, I have the same message.

"Why do we have to be there when we don't even live in the damn house?"

"It says something about a big donation she needs to talk to us about."

"Maybe they found out we swiped the paperwork for the Rolex Gredin gave. It did give us a big bump on the leaderboard."

"Whatever they say, you don't know shit about it and I don't know shit about it. We got each other's back, right?"

"You know it. And I know Gredin won't say anything."

"Speaking of Gredin, I've been thinking of a plan on how we can see him and Trip again."

"No way. I'm over it."

"You lie, but I'll let it slide. Take one for the team."

"Okay, let's hear it."

"That didn't take a lot of persuading." She side-eyes me.

"Oh, shut up."

'I DON'T know if this plan you've cooked up is going to work, Dericka," I tell her on the way over to Alpha Psi.

"It'll work. Trust me."

"Every time you say that I end up screwed... literally."

"And you're complaining?"

"No."

"Good. Then leave it to me. Operation: McEwen Brothers Fuck Day Take-Two is in full effect."

"Oh, man."

We walk into the house to see most of the girls in the living room watching a movie.

"There you are," Cierra says, having everyone turn in our direction.

"She did it," Dericka says, pointing at me.

"Are you serious? What happened to us not knowing shit and having each other's backs?"

"You know I choke under pressure."

"So, I guess Nichole is the one that's going to get the Cancun trip," Cierra says.

"Wait, what are we talking about?" Dericka asks.

"Gredin McEwen's donating a 1950s Porsche to go along with the Rolex he gave and his brother is donating a brand spanking new Escalade. They credited both of you, but if it was just Nichole—"

"No, no, no," Dericka says. "I was joking. Right, Nichole?"

"Mm-hmm," I say, resisting the urge to throw her ass under the bus.

"We already have the paperwork for the cars signed. They're requesting for you guys to pick them up tomorrow. Katie's dad says we can use his flatbed tow truck if you guys can't—"

"No, no. We can do it," Dericka tells her.

"Are you sure? Because if you get even a scratch on those cars the value will go way down." She hesitates before handing her the contact information and directions.

"It's not that far. We're good. We got it," Dericka says, trying hard not to snatch the paper from her.

"Cool," she says, handing it over. "Now, let's get this meeting started." She turns back to the other girls. "First on the agenda. Who left the used tampon on the bathroom sink?"

I eye Dericka, silently thanking God we don't live here.

DERICKA HOLDS our front door open while I walk in behind her. We were in the mood for spaghetti so we're cooking tonight. We stopped to pick up a bottle of wine to go with it.

"Should we chill the wine?" she asks, searching the bottle for directions on chilling it. She gives up and just shoves it in the freezer. "The McEwen influence," she says with a laugh.

"I know, right? But I'm sure we would have discovered how good it is eventually."

"Yep."

"Hey, do you think they're doing this car donation thing just to see us again?" I ask her.

"Hell yeah. I can't believe they beat us to it. I guess we rocked their worlds. This is much better than that stupid plan I came up with."

"You were all into that plan."

"I was horny. You know I can't think straight when I'm dick-deprived."

"Truth."

CHAPTER EIGHT
Nichole

"YOU WEREN'T kidding," Dericka says when we enter the lobby with that big fountain in the middle. "All he needs is the little orange men running around here breaking into song."

"I know," I laugh.

We stop by the lobby and we're directed up to Gredin's office where we're allowed to go right in. Both he and Trip are waiting for us.

"There they are," Trip says.

"In the flesh," Dericka says to him with the stupidest grin on her face. I roll my eyes at her before looking at Gredin who's smirking at me.

"Thank you for donating," I tell them, trying to keep some semblance of professionalism.

"It's truly our pleasure," Gredin says.

"And speaking of pleasure," Trip says. "What do you say we take a look at the Escalade, Blondie?" He tugs at one of her twists and I'm shocked she doesn't say anything about it. She's really into him.

"Lead the way," Dericka says, practically bouncing out the door with him.

The air is thick now that we're alone. I shift my weight from one foot to the other. The fact that he's just standing there staring at me isn't helping much.

"I want to thank you for— "

Before I can finish the sentence, he has me pinned against the wall.

"You already thanked me."

"True, but you never can be too thankful."

"I don't disagree. However, I'd much rather you show me exactly how thankful you are."

My breath hitches when he leans his hands on the wall on both sides of my head, trapping me against it. Before I can do anything, the door flies open and Dericka rushes in. She runs right past us before she can stop herself. Her head swivels in all directions looking for us until she spins around to where we are.

"Trip and I want to take the Escalade for a spin can we have the keys, please? He said they were up here with you." I grin at Gredin as he looks at me. He pushes himself off the wall and goes to get her the keys. She's fidgeting and twirling her hair, reeking of someone who's about to get laid. "Thanks," she says before squealing. Taking the keys from Gredin, she skips toward the door. "See you later, Nikki."

I shake my head as she leaves. She never calls me Nikki.

Gredin takes a step towards me once she's gone, only to be stopped by the sound of who I think is his assistant buzzing in telling him his dad wants to talk to him.

"I have to take this," he says, finally reaching me. "Don't go anywhere." He goes so far as to lock the door with a code. I only nod. It's not like I can now anyway.

Gredin

I GO into the conference room of my office to take the call.

"Dad?"

"Sorry about last night, son," he says about not returning my call. "I had way too much to drink."

"It's okay. I just wanted to ask you about that chocolate cake Mom gave to Trip."

"She did that to keep me from eating it. Did you like it?"

"Loved it. He said you got it from someplace in Alabama. Can you tell me where exactly?"

"Oh, I wish I could. A customer came into the store and was talking about ordering one last Thanksgiving. She made them sound so good I ordered a couple. We ended up freezing them until I fished them out a few days ago. I proudly ate half of one all by myself. My sweet tooth knows no bounds. By the way, we just got another shipment of fresh lobster in if you're interested."

"I am. I'll have Rhoda pick some up. How did you order them? The cakes I mean."

"I called her up. Told her where to send them."

"Do you still have the number?"

"No, I don't. I wish I did, now that I know how good they are."

"Can I find the place on the internet?"

"No, nothing like that. It's just a sweet old lady taking phone orders."

"What was her name?"

"It was something like Pearl or Lynn maybe." *Shit, that could be anyone.* "Is this about the launch? Tripper told me you were worried about it."

"Worried? You mean about the launch we've hyped up for a non-existent cake? Absolutely nothing to worry about."

"You're putting too much pressure on yourself. It can't be that hard to make a cake."

"With our temperamental chocolate, it's damn near impossible."

"Maybe your granddad can help. It's his chocolate after all."

"Dad, I'm not calling him out of retirement to save my ass. This whole thing was my idea so it's on me. I need to figure it out."

"You're as stubborn as he is and just as determined so I'm sure you will. Call your grandfather if you need him. He'll be happy to help."

"I will. If you can think of anything else about that baker let me know."

"Will do."

I REENTER my office, finding Nichole out on the terrace admiring the view. My head is pounding from this impending disaster I've created. I need to be balls deep inside her to relieve the pressure.

I creep up behind her, running my hands up the bare skin of her legs. I can feel her body shudder when I lift her skirt. I only get it up mid-thigh before she stops me.

"I won't bite," I say, but I'm sure she doesn't believe that for a minute.

My mouth's at her ear. She squirms away until she feels my lips on the back of her neck. She leans over the rail to give me better access to it, all the while reaching back to grab my ass, pulling me closer.

Turning her around, I kiss her. My tongue dances deliciously with hers. Damn, she tastes good. I pick her up and spin us around. With her feet back on the ground, I walk her backward inside the office.

"Fuck," I whisper when she works the buttons of my shirt, tossing it to the floor. I return the favor, undoing her blouse and slipping it off. "Mmm," I growl at the cranberry lace bra she has on.

When the backs of her knees hit the edge of the couch, her lips leave mine as she goes over it. I come down on top of her. She wiggles her way up the couch and lands with a thud at the other end of it. I'm still right on top of her with my mouth finding her again. My hands are all over her smooth skin. Her hands are on my shoulders pushing me off.

I give her enough room so that she can position herself on top of me. She kisses her way down my body and I lift my hips so she can slide off my pants. She dips her hands into my boxer briefs, freeing my cock to stroke it.

"Fuck," I hiss when she takes me into her mouth and sucks me hard.

"Who was that girl in that picture with you on the Internet? The one with that jawbreaker stuck between her teeth?" She pops me out of her mouth to ask. "Girlfriend?"

"She wants to be." I strain to speak because she's sucked me back in her mouth again. "Shit, you're fucking good at that."

"Are you going to let her?" She stops again to ask me.

"Are you torturing me with good head so that I'll have a reason not to?" She makes her eyebrows dance as she sucks me harder. "Pretty Nikki, which one of you has my cock in her mouth, and which one has a jawbreaker?"

"But that doesn't mean anything," she takes me out to say.

"Yes, it does." She takes me back in again. "Don't stop," I demand, so she continues to suck me off. I stop her only when I'm oozing with precum. "I almost came."

"Which would have been fine with me."

"I want to fuck you."

She crawls off me and onto the thick rug on the floor.

I join her, but not before toeing out of my shoes and taking off my pants and boxers.

I help her out of her heels and her cranberry lace panties, a perfect match to the bra she still has on. Now on top of her, I pull the cups of it down, exposing her tits.

"Shit," I say looking at them, kneading them with the palms of my hands, feeling the nipples get hard from my touch. I take one in my mouth and suckle.

Her back arches in response. Her hands are in my hair, pulling me into her before I move on to the other nipple.

I hike her skirt up, ready to fuck her but freeze.

"Fuck, fuck, fuck, no condom," I say. I never replaced the one I used when I fucked her the first time. She wiggles underneath me and I lift enough for her to grab one from her bag on the coffee table. "I won't bother asking why the fuck you're carrying those in there."

"Why not?"

"Because right now, whatever the reason is, it wouldn't stop me from fucking you."

She squeezes her hands between us and slides on the thin rubber that would soon be the only thing separating us.

"Oh, God," she says when I slide into her. She disengages her hands from where they still were between us and grabs my ass. The feel of my dick inside her is almost too much for me to take.

It's like her pussy was made for me. The way it's massaging my dick tells me I'm hitting her sweet spot. I'm hitting her so good it's making her wet. She's fucking drowning me. The squishing sounds her pussy is making as I pound into the pool I'm creating has her turning away from me.

"Don't do that," I say.

"I'm sorry I'm so wet."

"Are you kidding me?" I moan, pounding into her harder. "You feel so fucking good. Tight and wet and addictive." That's all the encouragement she needs. She shifts her body weight. Understanding immediately, I shift with her, lying on my back and pulling her on top of me. "Shit," I say as she works her hips, riding me.

I circle her back, bringing her down flat on my chest. Her teeth sink a little into my shoulder to keep from crying out as she comes. Her orgasm comes pouring out of her. After a few more strong pumps I spill myself into the condom.

What I wouldn't have given for it to be me spilling out in her and feeling her warm juices around me without the condom in the way.

But the way it is now is fucking amazing.

Her body is completely still. Her nose is on my shoulder but she replaces it with her lips, sucking on the place where she bit me.

I promised her I wouldn't bite. In hindsight, I should have made her do the same. I'm glad I didn't though. It made me come harder.

I kiss the side of her head and run my hands down her back until she stands up.

I smirk with pride at the sight of her juices dripping from between her legs as she stands spread eagle over me. I watch as she bites her lip, tugging her skirt down. Damn, I love her mouth. She truly is a biter. She reaches her hand out to me and I grab hold of it, allowing her to help me up.

She moves into me; her head is resting on my shoulder and her arms are wrapped around my waist. She fits perfectly and my body must think so, the way my muscles react to her touch.

I wrap my arms around her neck, enjoying the feel of her. We stay in each other's arms for God knows how long until with one final peck on my shoulder, she lets me go.

Nichole

"DO YOU want anything to eat or drink? I meant to ask you back when you came in, but you distracted me."

"How did I do that?"

"By walking into the room."

"Oh," I say with a little laugh. I go about the room picking up my things. I seem to be doing this a lot when I'm with him. "No, I'm okay. I really should get home."

"Are you trying to fuck and duck me? I don't know if I should be impressed or insulted."

"What? No. I have a sketch to do for class in the morning and I haven't even started."

"Is it something perverse?"

I smile, remembering our first conversation.

"I wish. But my professor is a dud. I have to sketch nature and give my opinion on the La Brea Tar Pits."

"What's your conclusion?"

"They're beautifully done. But sad. I love elephants." I pause, looking him up and down. "I can't believe I'm having such a regular conversation after what we just did. It seems afterglow makes me ramble."

"A happy byproduct of fucking."

"I guess so. At least I didn't lose my panties this time."

"Damn. I'm off my game."

"And why were you so pissed at me that night? I thought we had a good time."

"We did and I wasn't pissed at you. I was pissed at the thought of men fucking you. It wasn't something I wanted to hear."

"Well, it wasn't like I was going to go right out after fucking you to fuck someone else."

"I didn't want to know about it if you were."

"Good because when I do, I have no intentions of ever telling you."

"Wait a second. Who else are you planning to fuck?"

"None of your business. A few of my best orgasms might belong to you but *I* don't."

"Just a few huh? I'll have to work on that. In the meantime, let me take you home."

"No, it's fine."

"You don't want me to know where you live?"

"Is that *required* with fucking and ducking?"

"Touché," he smirks. "Speaking of fucking and ducking, why do you have condoms in your bag?"

"I thought you didn't care to know."

"I changed my mind."

"Not that I owe you an explanation, but it's Dericka's doing. She puts them in everything. Even made me practice putting it on a banana to make sure I did it right. She likes being overly prepared."

"Well, thank fuck for overly prepared roommates."

"You got that right. Anyway, I have a Porsche to drive, remember?"

"Actually, I forgot."

"It's not a stick shift, is it?"

"No," he says, rubbing his forehead like it hurts.

"You okay?"

"Just a long day which is shaping up to be a part of a very stressful Valentine's Day that I'm not prepared for."

"Are you seriously telling me that Mr. Candy is not ready for a candy day?"

"Mr. Candy?"

"Dericka's name for you."

"I like it."

"You would. What has you so stressed? I've tried your chocolates and you have nothing to worry about."

"It's not the chocolates. Not the chocolate candy anyway. I'm branching the company out into desserts and we were scheduled to launch a cake using our signature chocolate. I've spent a fortune on the factories and the equipment, not to mention marketing."

"Yeah, your ads keep popping up all over my social media. Just looking at that cake makes my mouth water."

"Well, let's just say the taste is falling short. I have a few days to correct it before it all goes to shit."

"And here I am taking up all of your time."

"You've been a very pleasant and much-needed distraction. I enjoy you hopping around in my head."

"Well, dip me in your chocolate and I can be your sweet little bunny."

"Wrong holiday, baby. Although, you're giving me ideas. You'll taste good dipped in chocolate."

"Ha. Good luck making that happen. We are one and done."

"That was three fucks ago. But who's counting."

"It looks like we are."

"In that case, care to make it four?"

"In your dreams."

"You're feisty when you're sexually satisfied."

"That's some ego you've got there. You think you did all that?"

"I *know* I did all that and I prefer to call it my animal instinct."

"Well, seeing as how you're the only animal that's ever mounted me, I don't have anything to counter you with so I'll just shut up."

"Let's keep it that way."

"What do you mean?"

"I don't want you fucking anyone else."

"Why?"

"Because I want to fuck you again. I have a lot going on right now. The last thing I want to do is put you on the back burner, but something's got to give."

"So, I'm supposed to sit around and wait for you to be free to fuck me again."

"Not sit around. We'll still talk. I'm not going to disappear on you, but yes, wait for me to fuck you."

"Dericka might have a say in that. She likes to fuck me."

"She doesn't have a dick so it doesn't count."

"You realize you just insulted a whole community of lesbian women."

"They can go fuck themselves and Dericka can fuck you. Just not with a dick. On second thought, she still gives you orgasms and I don't want her to have those."

"Boy, you are something else. What about your fucking and ducking one-and-done thing?"

"Let's make it a month and done or at least until Valentine's Day. A sweet November, if you will."

"It's February."

"Even better. All the more reason to woo you."

"Woo me. How old are you?"

"Old enough to know better but still young enough not to give a fuck."

"You better give a fuck. A *really* good one."

"As soon as I get this cake debacle under control."

"Okay. I'm game." It's not like I have any other prospects at the moment, but he doesn't need to know that.

"That's my pretty little Nikki bunny."

"Hop, hop." I make bunny paws with my hands while I bounce up and down.

He shakes his head with a grin as he goes over to his desk and comes back with the keys to the Porsche. He escorts me down to the parking garage to a very dirty car.

"I told my idiot brother to have the damn thing detailed."

"No worries. We're having a car wash on Saturday so this is perfect."

"You're a resourceful bunch."

"Don't let it fool you. It's just an excuse for us to wear bikinis and get wet. Fingers crossed that it's as hot as predicted, otherwise we'll all catch pneumonia."

"Anything for charity." He holds the door for me to get in.

"Right."

I start her up and she purrs like a kitten. I stick my hand out the window and wave right before I pull out into traffic.

CHAPTER NINE

Nichole

TRUE TO his word, Gredin was busy the whole week. Also true to his word, he found time for me. He'd do things like take his lunch at the same time I had mine so we could facetime while we ate, but mainly it was through late-night phone calls.

I've never talked to a guy so long without it ending up with him trying to get between my legs, but Gredin has already been there and he still called me every night just to talk. He's been so easy to talk to. I told him things I rarely ever talked about or even said out loud and he wanted to hear about them.

"So, both your parents are bohemians?" he asked me.

"I think it's more Dad's influence. Mom wanted to be an educator. She met him when she was a freshman at Alabama State. She was at a burger stand and he asked to draw her. He wasn't from there. He was passing through *on his way to Florida. She said she'd never seen anything like him. He swept her off her feet and I was born a few months later. He calls her his muse. Next to Mom, art is his passion."*

"I guess it runs in your blood."

"Probably, but I don't think I had much of a choice. Mom says the minute I came out of the womb, he put a paintbrush in my hand. I spent more time in art museums than I did in school. They were also into RVing before it became a thing. We lived in an old Winnebago that kept breaking down on the side of the road. My grandparents were not impressed."

"Is that why you went to live with them?"

"I think my grandmother threatened to grab custody. Mom and Dad were great but I was definitely lacking adult supervision growing up with them. They were still kids themselves, really. They dropped me off at my grandparents' house when I was about seven."

"Did you see them often?"

"All the time. I used to travel with them on my summer vacations before I came here to school."

"Who did you like living with more?"

"I love my mom and dad but home has always been with my grandparents. They'd wake up at six every morning. You could set your watch to it. I remember being in bed, snug and warm under thick blankets in the winter, listening to them move around the house. My grandfather Willie would get the fireplace going so the house would be warm for me when I got up. Before long, the smell of

delicious breakfast being cooked by my grandma would hit my nose. I can almost smell it now."

"It sounds comforting."

"It was. It took a lot for me to get on that plane and leave them to come out here."

"I have to admit that I, for one, am glad you did."

"Me too. What about you? Have you always lived in LA?"

"Born and raised. My parents divorced when I was fourteen so I spent my time living with my mom in San Diego and my dad here in Beverly Hills. The only break from that was when I would spend time at my grandfather's cacao farm in Hawaii."

"He taught you everything you know?"

"He did and he was relieved that someone in the family other than him loved it. From the time he gave me my first chocolate bar, I was obsessed with learning how to make it. So, he showed me."

"I can't believe something as wonderful as chocolate comes out of those nasty-looking pod... things. What are they anyway?"

"Seeds and I said the same thing at first. But seeing my grandfather cultivate them made me appreciate it."

"So, I guess chocolate is in your blood."

"It is. I can't tell you how many times I walk the farm with him. I think the man knows every tree personally."

"That's probably why it's so good. See, now you have me craving it."

He sent some over after he finagled my address out of me. It was worth it because not only did he send me pounds of decadent chocolate but a basket of the most deliciously gourmet heart-shaped suckers I'd ever had. They were huge, like the kind you get from amusement parks. There had to be over a hundred of them so I shared with the girls at the sorority house.

Now every time I stop by, I find one or two squirreled away somewhere. I don't know why they're hiding them from each other. They can open a candy store with the amount of them they have. I remember Gredin telling me about how he came up with the recipe. Up until that point, I had no idea there was so much to it. I thought a sucker was a sucker. I used to make them all the time as a kid. All you have to do is heat some sugar and add a little food color and flavoring. That's exactly what I told him and I have yet to live it down. He sure set me straight.

"*Think back to when you were a kid,*" he said. "*What was your favorite sucker?*"

"*Blow Pops. They had gum in the middle so it was like a twofer.*"

"*Which was your favorite flavor?*"

"*Green apple.*"

"*Okay, now think back to all the other green apple suckers you've had. Did they taste anything like the Blow Pop one; even though they were the same flavor?*"

"*Nope. Nothing like it.*"

"*You would know that green apple sucker anywhere, wouldn't you?*"

"*Now that you mention it. It is very distinctive.*"

"*Exactly. There's a science in creating shit like that.*"

"Well, damn."

It's true what they say. You learn something new every day.

I HOLD up one of the suckers for Dericka to see as I walk into the common area of the Alpha Psi house. We're waiting for the car wash to kick off.

"Where'd you find that one?" she asks.

"In the damn bathroom."

"What the hell were they doing with it in there?"

"Ew," I say, tossing it on the couch next to where she's sitting. Why did she have to ask me that? I can only imagine what they were doing with it.

"No respect for candy." She shakes her head at it.

"Nasty asses." I disgustingly wipe my hand on what little fabric I have on my swimsuit.

We hear the unmistakable sound of horns and engines coming down the street.

"Let's do this," Dericka says.

She slips out of her cover-up to show off that thing she calls a bikini. Both of her ass cheeks are out. I don't know how she got away with wearing that, but she does look good.

WE'RE TWO hours into this four-hour car wash and I think we've washed about a thousand cars. We're doing a shitty job of it too. Mostly just playing with the water and flashing boob. I bitched about it to Dericka, thinking people spent good money and we're not delivering the service, but she set me straight.

"Look around," she said. "There's nothing but horny guys in line. "You think they care about getting their car cleaned? They came to see tits and ass so just go with it."

She was all good until I pointed out that Trip was in the line. He was getting his car washed by Meesha who was getting herself off on his hood. The only thing I could see of Trip was his damn teeth. He was eating that shit up. I was going to hold Dericka back but I knew not to get in her way when she kicked off her flip-flops.

Two of the girls had to break up the catfight when Dericka pulled Meesha down by her weave. She was going after Trip next but he had sense enough to drive away.

"What happened to just going with it?" I ask when she comes back over like she didn't just beat somebody down.

"I saw Gredin a few cars back. Let's see how *you* go with it."

"Oh, hell no." I toss the hose I was using. Trina yells when the nozzle hits the ground and sprays water on her hair. If she says one word to me about it later, I'll choke her ass out with that damn hose.

I glare at Gredin through his passenger-side window before hopping in. I forget all about how wet I am.

"What?" he asks. He barely glances at me for the second it takes him to speak. He's too preoccupied with watching two girls wet his car down.

"Seriously. What the hell are you doing here?"

"I came to see you."

"I'm over here," I say. He finally looks over with a stupid smirk on his face. "Get off the hood!" I yell at a girl, snapping my fingers at her to shoo her away. The bitch isn't even in our sorority. It only makes him smirk harder. "I cannot *believe* you showed up for this."

"I wouldn't have missed it. Seeing you in this is worth it." He pops the hip strap of my burnt orange bikini. "I love this color on you." He slides his hand between my thighs. "Mmm, wet and slippery." The way he growls at me gets me even wetter.

The fact that he's now bulging out of the shorts he's wearing isn't helping the situation any.

"That hard-on better be for me."

"Was it here when you first hopped in?"

"No."

"Then, it's only for you, baby."

"I... uh," I say, nodding my head toward his crotch. "I better get back out there before I rip those off you and take what's mine."

"I sure as hell wouldn't stop you."

"And give my house mother a heart attack. She's already trying to douse holy water on us now."

The rich baritone of his laughter has my body tingling. I chalk it up to not having orgasms. I was a damn fool for agreeing to only let him be the one to give them to me. Now I'm at his mercy.

"We're still on for tonight?" he asks.

Yes!

"Are you sure you can break away?" I try to play it off like I'm not eager to get laid. "I know you're down to the wire."

"Absolutely. I want to see you."

"Okay, and I have a little surprise for you." I say it like it's nothing, but I've been thinking about it for a while now.

"Really?"

"Definitely."

"I can't wait."

"See you tonight," I tell him, hopping out. I do a bunny hop, watching him laugh as he drives away.

"You are *sooo* gone," Dericka says when I get back to her.

"You're one to talk."

I'VE BEEN looking forward to tonight since Gredin drove away from the car wash but I dare not tell Dericka that. She already thinks I'm too hung up on him. Nothing could be farther from the truth. Don't get me wrong, he's okay to hang out with, but that's about as far as it goes. Telling myself that hasn't stopped me from being nervous about tonight though. It feels like a date.

It is definitely, most certainly not a date.

"Oh, it's not?" Dericka asks.

"Did I just say that out loud?"

"Yep."

"Doesn't matter. It's true."

"Right. Well, it may not be a date but that's not stopping you from checking yourself out in whatever object has your reflection in it," she says.

"Shut up," I say, catching myself in the toaster.

My hair is in a ponytail but I have a flyaway strand sticking out the side of my head. No matter how much product I put in to slick it down I always have that damn flyaway. My grandmother says it's my antennae. I still brush it back with my hand a few times.

"Your hair is fine. Relax."

"I *am* relaxed," I say before moving on to tidying up the kitchen for the third time.

"Are you sure about this?" Dericka asks as she looks at the chocolate cake on the counter.

"Why not? After all, it's his commercials that made me want to make it in the first place. I think he'll like it."

"He'll *love* it, but it's your grandmother's secret recipe."

"I'm not giving up the recipe. I just want to inspire him."

"Oh, that will certainly inspire him if he can get past that dress you're wearing."

It's a burnt orange mini dress I bought earlier today because he said he liked the color on me.

"I *do* look good. Don't I?"

"Bitch, you look smoking hot." I glance toward the door when we hear the bell ring. "I got it." She hops off the bar stool. I hear him greet her but I can't make out what else is being said. "I'm out," she yells to me before leaving.

"Sorry to keep you waiting," I say, coming out of the kitchen. "I was just checking on your surprise."

"You mean I have another surprise besides this dress," he says, growling as he grabs me and pulls me into him.

His hands are all over me and his nose is running up my neck, smelling me. I do the same to him. He smells yummy.

It took me an hour to get ready but it takes him only five minutes to have me undressed, with my hair messed up, and my lipstick smeared. It takes him about ten minutes after that to have me screaming his name and coming so hard I see stars.

"Fuck, I needed that," he breathes.

I stay trying to calm down for a good five minutes before I can talk.

"Hard week?" I finally say, turning over on my side to look at him.

"Let's not talk about it. I don't want to ruin the high or my *other* surprise."

"Well, talking about it is sort of keeping with the theme of the surprise."

He stares at me while I stare at him.

"Are you going to make me guess what it is?" he asks.

"Why don't I just show you."

"Even better."

Getting out of bed proves harder than I thought. My legs are weak. Damn, he wore me out. I finally get myself together and slip on my robe while he slips on his boxer briefs. He does this thing where he scratches the back of his leg and I have to roll my eyes at myself because it turned me on. He pauses at the door, stepping aside so I can go ahead of him. I slide by, walking through the living room then planting him in a seat at the dining room table.

"So, I'm guessing you're still not happy with the cakes your bakers are sending out."

"You'd be right."

"Okay, give me a minute." I disappear into the kitchen and come back with the cake. "Before you say anything, I know you're probably drowning in these, but this one is just to give you an idea."

"You baked this?" he asks when I set it down on the table, sliding over one of the plates that was preset.

"Guilty."

"For me?"

"Of course, for you, silly."

"You are incredible."

"True. But you should taste it before you sing my praises." I cut him a slice and place it on his plate. I watch as he picks up his fork to take a bite.

"I'm sure I'll love it," he says right before eating it. I hold my breath as he chews. I know it's good. I've been practicing the recipe for the last two days, but I don't know if he'll think it's good enough to try and replicate. My worry is put to rest when his eyes light up. "Baby," he says, before eating another forkful. "Jesus."

"You like it?"

"I fucking love it. It's the best damn cake I've ever had."

"You're exaggerating."

"About chocolate cake? Never. I mean every word."

"Really? Because I know it's not 'earth's best' or whatever but I was thinking that maybe your people could make something similar. Put your company's signature spin on it."

"With your direction, they most certainly could."

"My direction?"

"On how to make it."

"You want *me* to direct your people? *Me*?"

"My connoisseurs and absolutely yes you."

"Connoisseurs. That means they studied to do this stuff. I don't know *anything* about baking. You have to be playing with me."

"I'm serious, and they may have studied but they sure as hell can't make this cake taste like you just did so you know more than they do. I would love to hire you to—"

"Hire me. But I just followed the recipe."

"Whose recipe?"

"My Grandma Pearline. She gave it to me to make for Dericka on Valentine's Day. I told her how your commercials had me craving it. She was going to ship me one from Alabama, but I wanted to make it."

"Wait a minute. Pearline… from Alabama?"

"The very one."

"She makes the best cakes in the entire state?"

"You better believe it."

"All from right out of her little kitchen. Doesn't even have a website."

"Nope. She's not into computers. It's all word of mouth. And how do you know all of that? I sure didn't tell you."

"You won't believe me but Trip's mom let me taste one of your grandmother's cakes. I've been trying to find her ever since."

"To buy another one?"

"Not just one. All of them. I want to buy the right to mass produce it."

"Whoa, Gredin, I don't know. That recipe has been in our family for generations."

"I understand that better than anyone and I completely respect it. I'm not trying to change it or do anything you wouldn't approve of."

"Hmm."

"Baby, I'm sure we can work something out."

"I can't make any promises. My grandmother can be very stubborn so don't get your hopes up."

"I won't. Just let me talk to her."

"Right now?"

"Time is of the essence."

"Give me a minute." I get my phone from the counter and check the time even though I know whatever time it is she's still up. The woman rarely sleeps. I go into my bedroom to talk to her.

"Baby, what are you still doing up?"

"It's not that late here, Grandma."

"Yeah, but I thought you had a date with Mr. Candy."

I groan. Why do I tell her these things?

"Uh, well that's actually why I'm calling. Long story short, I baked him one of your chocolate cakes and he loves it."

"Of course, he does."

"So much so that he wants his company to sell it. Grandma?" I call her after she's quiet for too long.

"Are you telling me this man wants to sell my cakes in the grocery stores? Under his brand?"

"Yes, Ma'am."

"I'm going to be famous? Like Famous Amos or Patty Labelle and her pies. Little ol' Pearline Adams from Selma, Alabama is about to have her face in the local Walmart. Wait until I tell your great aunt Maybelle about *this*. I told her I would make it big with these cakes one day. Had the nerve to call me crazy."

"Wait, you've wanted to do this? I thought you just liked baking."

"I love it, but I don't like baking so many cakes."

"Why make so many?"

"Baby, how do you think we paid for this house after the mill closed down? I had to bake."

"But Grandma, I don't think it would be like having your face in Walmart. I think he wants to buy the recipe from you so he can just make them himself."

"So, no life-sized cutouts of me holding the cake in the dessert aisles?"

"Afraid not."

"I'm okay with that. How much is he offering to pay?"

"He didn't say and I didn't feel right talking to him about it when it should be you."

"I understand, baby. Go ahead and hand him the phone. Let me talk to that man."

"Okay, hold on." I go back into the dining room. "She wants to talk to you," I tell him before putting her on speaker. "Okay, he's here."

"Hello, Mr. Cand... I mean... uh..."

"Oh, God," I groan. This is not how I pictured these two meeting.

"Call me Gredin, ma'am."

"Nice to meet you, Gredin. You can call me Pearline. Everybody else does."

"Pearline."

"Now that that's out of the way, let's talk business," she says. She doesn't miss a beat and Gredin's grin tells me he likes that. "My grandbaby says you want to buy my cake recipe."

"That's right. I don't know how much Nichole has told you but I've been searching for the perfect recipe for some time now and I believe yours is it."

"You know it won't come cheap."

"How does forty thousand dollars sound?"

I nearly choke on my own spit when he asks her that.

"For a cake recipe. Oh, I'm sure it's a little more to it than that." She sounds completely unfazed and I'm shocked by how cool she is. "What's the catch?"

"The offer comes with urgency. Nothing more. Quite frankly, under normal circumstances, I would sell you on the reputation that comes with my name and the way my company does business, but as it stands, I'm running out of time so you have me over a barrel. Whatever your price, I think you know as well as I do that I'll still come out on top if I had the recipe for that delicious cake."

"No truer words have ever been spoken."

"I just have one concern."

"What's that?"

"Do you think it would incorporate well with my chocolate?"

"It should since your chocolate is what I use. I know you're in a hurry but I need to have it all spelled out for me in writing."

"I would expect nothing less."

"If you can get me something by tomorrow, I'll have my great-nephew look it over."

"Sammy?" I ask her.

"He's coming to have Sunday dinner with me. He's a corporate lawyer down there in Florida." She says that part for Gredin's benefit. "Text him my information, baby, so he'll know where to send it."

"Okay," I say with a shake of my head. I never thought she'd know about texting.

"And I'll send it right over to you first thing in the morning," he tells her.

"I look forward to hearing from you, Gredin."

"Bye, Grandma."

"Bye, baby."

No sooner does the call end than Gredin has me in his arms spinning me around.

"You're a lifesaver." He puts me down.

"All I did was bake a cake."

"You did so much more than that and you know it."

The quick peck on the lips he tried to give me turns deeper. He unties my robe but I hold it closed.

"Don't you have to talk to your people about a proposal they need to get started on?"

"Right," he says. He's about to step back but he pauses, taking my face in his hands. I catch my breath watching him study me. So much is being said in the way he's looking at me. He kisses me again and it makes me weak in the knees.

"Proposal," I whisper, coming up for air. If he doesn't leave now, I won't be responsible for my horny actions.

"Right," he says again, going for the door this time.

I already have my phone out texting him the information before he even makes it to his car. I cross my fingers that it works out.

CHAPTER TEN

Nichole

I T TURNS out my grandmother wasn't as calm, cool, and collected as she appeared over the phone. She called me around midnight when it finally hit her.

"Do you think he's going to pay me that much for a cake recipe?"

"I don't think he would have said it if he wasn't prepared to do it. I just wonder what it means. Do you think it means you'll never get to make that cake again?"

"I'm sure I can make it. I just probably won't be able to sell it which is fine with me. I won't have to heat up the house so much this summer. Maybe I can focus on my garden. Keep my collard greens from wilting. Baby, I still can't wrap my mind around all of this. To think someone would pay that much for a chocolate cake recipe. The man is paying for his own chocolate. How bad do his bakers have to be that they can't come up with a cake using that man's chocolate."

"I know," I laugh.

"I wonder how much he'd pay for my caramel cake."

"Grandma!"

"What? You know I have a whole lot of recipes and can you believe I almost called that man Mr. Candy? I've never been so embarrassed in all my life."

"You're telling me."

SAMMY NEARLY broke his neck rushing to get Grandma to sign the contract Gredin sent over. Especially since he was able to negotiate her getting a percentage of the sales. If all goes well, in a few short days her cakes will be sold to chocolate lovers all over the world. I'm kind of sad that people won't know they're her cakes, but watching her spend that money will help ease the pain, I'm sure. She's not too worried about it. She says folks back home will only have to taste it to know it's her cake and I believe her too.

After everything was finalized, Sammy taught her how to facetime and she called me, popping open a bottle of champagne to celebrate.

Ironically, Gredin has me doing the same thing but I get to celebrate with him in person. He invited me to his cake factory for his soft launch today. It was technically supposed to be Grandma but she declined, saying that she didn't just get all that money only to die in a plane crash before she could spend a penny of it. She was shaking her lucky rabbit's foot all while she said it.

I'm impressed by the whole Earth's Best Chocolate operation. The chocolate makers have on the white baker's uniform with the tall white hat. It reminds me of watching the *I Love Lucy* episode with Grandpa Willie. The one where they're working at the chocolate factory.

I'm more impressed by Gredin. You can just see how much he loves what he does. He puts a lot of himself into not only his company but his brand. I can understand why he was stressing so much about the threat of failing it, and I can also see that Grandma's cakes are going to be in very good hands.

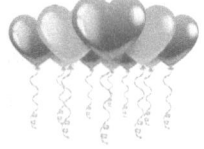

GREDIN, BEING much more relaxed after the launch party, has me hemmed up against my car in his parking garage. He's been thanking me for coming for the last twenty minutes. My car is running and the door is open. I have the AC on and even though the cool breeze is hitting my legs, it's doing very little to stop the heat that's coming from between them. Especially since I know the only thing stopping his hands from being there are the security cameras above us.

"What are you doing Valentine's Day?" he asks.

"I was supposed to be baking a cake for Dericka, but

now I'll just buy one of yours," I tease him. "And since we won the online auction, thanks to you and Trip, we'll be packing for a three-day vacay to Cancun."

"Exciting."

"Most definitely."

"You know what would be more exciting?"

"I'm listening."

"If you ditch Dericka and spend Valentine's Day with me."

"Hmm. That does sound exciting and I would but we have this whole hoes-before-bros pact going on and since her dickmance with Trip fizzled out she's moved on to her 'fuck men' stage."

"Make an exception. All in the name of our sweet November."

"It's February."

"All the more reason."

"I'll do it on one condition."

"I'm listening."

"You bring some chocolate to dip your bunny in."

"Oh, baby, you read my mind. I'll pick you up—"

"You know I prefer to drive."

"How could I have forgotten. I'll text you my address. Say around eight?"

"See you then." I slide into my car and take off for home before he can do anything more to me.

"NIK, IS that you?" Dericka asks.

"Yep, it's me."

I enter her room to find her in bed with a box of Gredin's chocolates.

"At least one McEwen is good for something," she says as I sit next to her. She holds the box in front of me so I can get one.

"Mmm. Mm-hmm," I say, eating it. "And he wants to see me on Valentine's Day."

"I figured he might."

"I can totally stay here with you."

"And have you bitch at me all while we're in Cancun. No thank you."

"No way. I wouldn't do that. Hoes before bros all the way."

"Girl, please. If it was me and Trip didn't run off with that skank Meesha, I'd leave your ass in a minute."

"You're such a bitch and a liar because you would not."

"True, but you need to. Besides, I want to be alone with my dildo. Why break the tradition, right."

"Dericka—"

"I mean it. I need to get my head together and that means swearing off men for this whack Valentine's Day. But when we get to Cancun, it's going to be on and crackin'."

"There's my girl."

"In the meantime, I hope all this candy goes straight to my thighs and tits 'cause I have this kick-ass bikini I need to fill out." She pops another chocolate in her mouth as I laugh.

"Let me get some wine so we can really thicken you up."

"Bring the bottle. I want to get *real* thick. Those Cancun boys aren't going to know what hit them when I touch ground."

"A whole damn hurricane."

"With no warning, baby."

VALENTINE'S DAY

"DAMN, YOU look hot," Dericka says.

"I better after all I went through," I tell her. "I've been primped, waxed, and my hair is even fried, dyed, and laid to the side. It's all topped off with a dusting of cara-mel-flavored lickable powder to compliment the chocolate Gredin *better* have waiting for me."

"I'm turned on just thinking about it. I hope I have enough extra batteries for this thing." She holds up her shiny silver vibrator.

"If not, check the top left drawer in my room. I have some stashed in there."

"Good looking out."

I make my escape from her room before she tries to rope me into a quickie. I grab the wine with the little red bow on it that I bought for tonight and head out.

"Don't wait up," I yell over my shoulder on the way out the door.

I DRIVE through the Holmby Hills a little scared at how tiny the streets are up here. I guess they need all the room for these massive houses. I find Gredin's place and thank God, he gave me access to his gate because there's nowhere to pull over and park legally up here. The last thing I need is a parking ticket.

I was right about them needing the room because his front lawn should be in a painting it's so big and beautiful. You'd have no idea it was waiting behind that monstrosity of a security gate. It's green and lush and edged to perfection. The house is nothing to sneeze at either, although it's not as big as I thought it would be. I can't tell if it's Spanish or Tuscan style but the design just screams Gredin McEwen lives here.

He told me to park right in front of the door so that's what I do. No sooner than he can get the front door open, he has me against the wall of his foyer with the palms of his hands on either side of my head to keep me in place.

"Have I told you how good you look tonight?"

"Twice in the last five minutes, but I would love to hear it again."

"You look phenomenal. Much too pretty to stay cooped up in here with just me. I'll take you out."

"It's crowded as hell out there. And you're looking much too good for me to share." I duck under his arm to escape him. "I thought of you when I saw this." I hand him the wine.

"Kincaid," he reads the name. "One of my favorites and I like the little red bow."

"I figured you might." I strut on into the living room without being asked.

The place looked small compared to his lawn but that's an illusion because once you get inside, it's massive. Most of the damn house is hanging over the edge of a hill or mountain or whatever it is. It's giving me a little bit of anxiety, and looking out at that infinity pool isn't helping the situation.

"Isn't the playboy mansion up here somewhere?" I turn around to ask him.

"Right next door."

"Oh, how convenient for you."

"Don't worry, baby. You're the only bunny I'm interested in. Make yourself at home. I'll be right back."

I nod and watch as he disappears into what I'm guessing is the kitchen because delicious smells of whatever we're eating come out of the door he opened and hit my nose. I take a look around, getting a feel of his place as I sit down. I'm always curious about being in someone else's home. My mom always says you can tell a lot about a person that way, and even though the space is big it feels warm and welcoming. It is very much lived in.

"I hope you're hungry," he says, reemerging.

He sits next to me and hands me a glass of the wine I gave him.

"Oh, don't worry. I brought my appetite," I say, taking it.

"Good. It'll be ready in a minute."

"Did you really cook for me?"

"Call me Mr. Kitchen," he says and I laugh.

"My grandmother is still embarrassed that she almost called you Mr. Candy."

"She shouldn't be. And with how she saved my ass, she can call me whatever she wants."

"How can you be so calm? Your cake has officially launched as of midnight last night. How are you not glued to your computer or phone checking on how it's doing?"

"It would be counterproductive at this point. It's out of my hands now and more importantly off my plate. The only thing I want to focus on tonight is you. A toast." He holds up his wine glass and I follow suit. "To Valentine's Day and it ending with my hands all over you."

I take a sip of wine to solidify his toast.

"And if you play your cards right, I just might come in them."

"Mmm," he says after tasting the wine. "I'm a gambling man and I can guarantee you compliment my tastebuds much more than this delicious wine."

"The way I'm seeping out of my panties, you're going to get more than just a taste."

"Show me." My brows crinkle in question. "Give me your panties."

The flicker in his eyes tells me he means it so I do as he says. Standing up, my hands disappear under my dress to slide my panties down. I lift one leg and then the other, taking them off and handing them to him, watching as he inhales the crotch. He catches me off guard when he sinks to his knees and grabs hold of my hips. I hold on to the tops of his shoulders to keep my balance. His head disappears under my dress. My head falls back at the feel of his tongue on my clit, tasting me. His crisp white shirt is a wrinkled mess in my hands.

"Oh, God," I scream as he flicks it to a hard nub, making me jerk forward with every swipe of his tongue. His head pops back out just when I'm about to come. "Why'd you stop!"

"I told you I was a gambling man. I just stacked the deck in my favor."

"Just for that, I'm going to make you work for it. Asshole."

"There's my feisty girl."

"Your feisty girl is hungry," I grumble.

"Say no more."

He gets up and leads me into the dining room. He slides my chair out, helping me to sit down before going into the kitchen.

"NEED ANY help?" I yell to him when I hear too many pots and pans being loudly handled.

"Just sit there and look pretty," he says. He emerges with two plates. "Lobster Bolognese with fresh capellini and brown butter truffle froth."

The way he announces it has me picturing one of those French chefs they used to have in the cartoons I'd watch as a kid.

"Mmmm smells delicious," I say when he sets my plate down.

"Wine," he says to himself before disappearing into the kitchen again.

I get the feeling he's not used to serving people. I bet he has a housekeeper or cook that normally does it. The fact that he's doing all of this for me makes me grin like a complete fool.

He comes back with the wine and two new glasses before he sits down.

"I'm feeling very spoiled," I say, watching him fill the glasses. I can't help but notice how those long fingers of his are wrapped around them.

I shake my leg to stop imagining him fucking me with one or two of them. He glances at me when he feels the table vibrating.

"That's the plan," he says, playing it off as he takes his seat. "I'm eager to know what you think of my cooking."

"Well, I'm not one to keep a gentleman waiting." I swirl some on my fork.

"Somehow I doubt that," he says.

I wink at his statement before eating.

"Mmm," I groan with satisfaction as I slide the fork out of my mouth. "*You* made this?" I ask as I chew.

"I did." He gives me a smug grin as he digs in and I

know a smart-ass comment is coming next. "I *do* have skills outside the bedroom."

There it is.

"I'm thoroughly impressed."

"And is it *seasoned* well?"

I have to stifle my laugh so I can swallow without choking. When he first told me he wanted to cook for me I joked about putting some Old Bay in my bag because the food would probably be unseasoned. I even threw in a jab about raisins in potato salad. I should have known he wouldn't let me get away with that.

"It's perfection. No Old Bay needed."

"Good," he says with a grin.

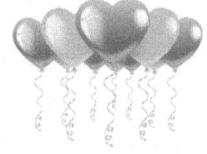

WHAT STARTED as me insisting on clearing the table ends up with me straddling him on his chair once I'm done.

"I like this lipstick," he mumbles, with my bottom lip caught between his teeth. He slides it out and smacks his lips to taste it. "What's it called?"

"Slut. Since I plan on being one tonight."

"A beautiful, sexy slut," he says nibbling my neck before moving to my ear. "Mmmm, your neck tastes delectable."

"I was hoping you'd like it."

"I love it."

"Are you still seeping for me, baby?"

"Only one way to find out."

With one quick motion, he lifts me and spreads me out on the table. I rest back on my elbows when he goes into the kitchen, waiting for him. He comes back in carrying a fancy jar. I watch as he grabs a napkin left on the table, shakes it out, then tucks a corner of it into his shirt, letting the rest hang like a bib.

"What are you doing?" I laugh.

"Having dessert."

He takes the jar out of its holder and hovers it over me. He pushes a little button on the side, and warm, milk chocolate comes drizzling out of it.

My eyes flutter closed at the feel of his hands running up my thighs as the chocolate sauce trickles down my pussy. I lay back in anticipation as I feel his mouth kissing my inner thigh. He doesn't make me wait long. He devours me like a man about to die of insulin shock.

"Damn, you're good at that," I breathe.

"Wait til you see what I do to you when a bed is involved."

"I don't think I can walk to it."

"Who said anything about letting you walk." He lifts me and carries me, along with the pretty jar of chocolate sauce, out of the dining room and up the stairs to his bedroom.

"Wow," I say, finding strength enough to leap out of his arms when I see the elaborate decorations.

Red long-stemmed roses are everywhere, filling the room with their fragrance, but not to be outdone are the deep red, heart-shaped balloons that are floating above us covering the entire ceiling. The soft, flickering light illuminating from the candles brings it all together. I twirl around once taking it all in before turning to him with my mouth open, unable to formulate a single word.

"Don't let the romance fool you into thinking this is going to be nice," he says. "I plan on fucking you senseless tonight."

"You still have to work for it and you messed up by giving me that orgasm because now I can hold out longer."

"We'll see about that." He sits on the edge of the bed and sits the jar in its holder on the floor beside him. He crooks his index finger at me. "Come here."

I stand in between his legs. He takes that same finger and traces the little blood-red hearts that are sewn into my black, Gothic-style corset dress before reaching behind me to unzip the back. He pretends not to notice when my belly sticks out as he does. I shrug. He's the one that just stuffed me full of lobster. I flinch a little when he pops me on my ass.

"I thought I already established who this belongs to."

"I think I need to be reminded."

He grabs me and tosses me to the side. I land on my back on the bed. He lifts my foot to take off my red-heeled sandal, only to let it drop so he can take off the other. I was preparing for him to drop that one but no such luck. The look in his eyes when he catches sight of the red toenail polish tells me I'm in big trouble.

"Slut?" he asks the color. With my lip stuck between my teeth to keep from laughing I just nod. I try to reclaim my leg but he holds on to it. "Mmm," he says, inhaling the sole of my foot. The feel of his nose on that sensitive spot is shooting straight between my legs.

He dips down and grabs the jar and drizzles a little chocolate on my foot. I whimper when he licks it off my big toe and then sucks it. My ass lifts off the bed I'm squirming so much.

If he keeps this up, I'm going to come.

He has the nerve to grin with three of my toes in his mouth. He's torturing me and he knows it. The asshole is enjoying it. I need to think of something to distract me. No way am I going to give him the satisfaction of coming *this* soon. But his warm mouth sucking on my toes is going to do me in. I really want to come.

Think of something else. Think of *anything* else.

How many licks does it take to get to the center—

No! Not that. That's making it worse.

I wonder if our dead relatives can see us fucking.

I picture my great grandma Gearline's mortified expression and it does the trick. My orgasm is nowhere to be found.

Okay, I'm good.

"You're really going to make me work for it, aren't you, baby?" He stops sucking long enough to ask me.

"You know it." I snatch my foot away before he can do anything else with it. I use my heels to scoot up on the pillows. "Are you sure this bed can take getting messed up by all this chocolate?"

"It's going to take a whole lot more than that before we're through."

"It's comfy," I say, caressing the sheet. "Much too big for me to be in here all by myself."

He sets the jar on the nightstand to undress. I lay back and enjoy the show. Even in the dim light, I can see his low tan line. Shorts must have been hanging off his ass while he was outside in the sun. My eyes follow the runway strip of hair that leads from his belly button down to his hard-on. The man is a paragon of perfection and he's all mine. At least for tonight. He climbs in next to me. He's on his back with his dick shooting straight up at the ceiling.

"Is that all for me?" I ask him.

"Every last inch. Now that you have his attention, what are you going to do with him?"

"Well, if I have his attention, he certainly deserves to have mine. Let me sweeten him up a little first."

I reach over him to grab the jar. My tits brush up against him. He darts his tongue out, trying to catch one of my rock-hard nipples but it's just shy of his mouth. I put a little of the chocolate sauce in my hand before setting the jar back down. Nestling myself between his legs, I slowly stroke the chocolate on. I grin at it sounding like the penis squishmallow toy Dericka brought me for Christmas last year. That sound coupled with Gredin's deep-throated moans is a turn-on.

He hisses when I lick the seam of his balls. The wrinkled skin is cool on my tongue. It's in total contrast to the taut, smooth skin of his dick. I lick up to the tip, circling my tongue around it before slurping it down. His precum is like whipped cream mixed with the chocolate sauce. Too bad The Coffee Hut isn't selling this concoction.

I pop him out with a grin. The skin is stretched so tight right now I can see the big blue pulsating veins.

"You're supposed to be working for it," I remind him when he starts to protest. Without a word, he grabs my arms and pulls me up, sitting me right over his face. "Oh, shit," I moan when his tongue fucks me so good my knees start to shake. There is no finesse in it. It's rough to the point that it's almost painful and he doesn't give a damn how hard he's doing it.

I'm pushing on his forehead to get him to stop but he's latched on like a damn leech determined to suck me dry.

Shit, shit, shit. I can't stop him. I can't stop myself from coming. I can't even think of anything to distract me. My entire body has become one big giant coiled-up clit. I'm on his face shaking like a rocket and my orgasm is ready to blast off.

"Oh, my God," I whisper, succumbing to it.

He lets go. He fucking stops.

"No, you don't," he says, smacking my thigh so hard it pisses me off.

"You did *not* just stop!" I feel like crying.

"Baby, you're not coming without me."

"Well, come on then."

With one final lick, he pulls me down and maneuvers me on the bed so that my back is to him. He yanks my leg up in the air and his dick is plunging inside me as he fucks me hard from behind. His thighs are slapping against the back of mine so hard it hurts. I try to steady myself by grabbing onto the closest thing, only to end up fisting the pillow and sheet.

It hurts so good I'm losing my whole mind.

My head is tilted back in the crook of his neck. His mouth is at my ear, sucking it, making me squirm. I feel it down to the tips of my toes. It gets me wet. So, so, so wet. I bite down on my lower lip to keep from telling him off when I feel him grin in smug satisfaction. I try to move my head but his arm snakes around my forehead, holding me in place. His tongue is flat on my neck, licking it before pressing his lips to my ear.

"Who does this tight, wet pussy belong to?"

"Oh, my God. You are *such* an asshole," I groan.

The breath from his chuckle tickles me.

"Do you *really* want to bring assholes into this, baby? Because I'm more than willing to accommodate—"

"Don't even think about it."

He bends my leg up higher, fucking me deeper, making me wetter. It's so thick that I can hear it when he slides in and out of me.

"Feisty. I'm going to fuck that out of you. Do you want that, baby? Do you want me to fuck that out of you? To fuck you like the slut that you are?" He runs his hands over my lips, smearing what's left of my lipstick. "The little slut that wore this just for me. Answer me."

"Yes."

"Yes, what?"

"Yes, I want you to fuck me. I want you to fuck the slut out of me."

"Do you deserve it?"

"Yes. I've been a really good slut."

"How bad do you want it?"

"So bad. I want it so bad."

"I know you do. I know you do. Whose slut are you?"

"I'm your slut."

"Don't ever fucking forget it."

"Never. Never. Oh, God. I need to come," I say, tapping out. "To hell with working for it."

He turns on his back, pulling me so that I'm flat on top of his chest. My head is resting on his shoulder and my legs are straddling him. I'm staring straight up at the ceiling as he pounds into my pussy from underneath me. One of his hands is splayed on my stomach, keeping me in place while the other is between my legs working my clit with his long fingers. I was bucking with him at first but now I can't move. My mouth is wide open but I don't even think I'm breathing anymore. My eyes are still fixated on the ceiling and I'm watching it get closer. If I could reach my hand up, I could touch the balloons. I can feel Gredin underneath me. His hands are still on me but I feel like I'm so far away from him.

"Breathe," he whispers in my ear and I hear myself gasp.

The sound brings me crashing back down into him.

"Oh, my God," I scream, feeling the full strength of coming. It's never been this strong before. I didn't think

it was possible. I'm convulsing violently on top of him.
I'm not sure I'm going to survive this one. Can people
die from orgasm?

"Fuck," he says.

He bites down on my shoulder to muffle the grunts of
him shooting his load off.

"I can't... I can't... I can't." I don't even know what I'm
trying to say so I shut up.

I'm just going to let whatever happens happen. If I die,
at least I died happy.

"Fuck, fuck, fuck," he breathes. "You are going to fucking kill me."

Look who's talking.

I'M LAUGHING for absolutely no reason and I've been
doing it for the past five minutes. I feel like I've had one
of Dericka's edibles. The ones that have way too much
weed but she insists they don't.

I'm next to Gredin in his bed with his cool sheet thrown
haphazardly over my legs. He's turned on his side with
his head jacked up on his pillow looking at me with a
cocky grin on his face that makes me laugh even harder.

"Condom!" I blurt out, coming down from my high.

"I have one on."

I peek down to see his dick still sheathed in the light-yel-
low latex with the tip full of his cum.

"When did you…? I didn't even see you put that on."

"While you were fucking my face."

"Oh, man," I laugh. "In my defense, at that moment, I wasn't thinking clearly. Thank you for remembering to protect me."

"I would never let you be unprotected, baby. Not even from me."

The gentleness in the way he says that is so out of character for him. I refuse to make any more of it than him just being a great lover on our final one and done.

CHAPTER ELEVEN

Nichole

WE SIT on the comfy couch in his bedroom showered and completely sated, polishing off the last of the wine and munching on chocolates.

"You've spoiled me," I tell him.

"You deserve to be spoiled on Valentine's Day."

"Before I met you, I was ready to screw the whole thing."

"I'm glad you screwed me instead."

"Even though I didn't make you work for it?"

"Believe me, I worked for it. It took everything in me to hold out until you came."

Now it's my turn to have a smug smile.

"Good, because you deserved it."

"And I enjoyed it. I also enjoyed being your first."

"You're going to be a hard act to follow." "Good. I want you to compare every limped dick, unworthy bastard that tries to fuck you to me."

"What for?"

"Because they won't be as good."

"And you're happy about that?"

"It's the perversion in me."

"You want me horny and miserably unsatisfied?"

"Not necessarily. I'd be more than willing to offer my services."

"Like rent-a-dick. I get to borrow it when needed."

"Sure, why not?"

"Oh no, it sounds good to me. Who am I to turn down good dick."

"Just good?"

"Gredin, I refuse to sit here and give you the satisfaction of bragging about your dick. No matter how spectacular it is."

"Define spectacular—"

"Don't push it."

"I wouldn't dream of it. So, perhaps when you get back from Cancun, we can pick this up again."

"Are you being serious?"

"Completely."

"Well, where else can this one-and-done take us?"

"For one, I can take you out on a date or two. We have a whole city to explore. And there's always *Netflix* and chill. After that," he shrugs, "we have many possibilities."

"I *love* possibilities."

"They are endless."

THREE HOURS and a strong cup of coffee later, I've been deemed okay to drive. That hasn't stopped him from holding me hostage for another thirty minutes with his tongue down my throat kissing me goodbye.

"I'll call you in three days," I tell him.

"You better."

I snicker.

"You sound like I'm fucking and ducking you. Like you're going to have my name on some website telling all the guys to watch out for me because I suck."

"Mmm, not a chance, baby." He smears my lipstick with his thumb. I just applied it before we walked out here. "I'm keeping this talented mouth and its sucking abilities all to myself."

"You are such an asshole," I laugh.

I kiss him, making it a really good one while slipping my tube of slut-red lipstick into his shirt pocket to re-member me by before sliding into my car. I'm careful not to crush the single rose I placed on the seat next to me. I wanted to take them all but I wouldn't have been home to enjoy them, so I made him promise to do it for me. I have most of the balloons in the back seat tied down so I can still see out of the back window.

He waits for it to heat up and I wait until he steps safely away before I pull off, blowing him a kiss goodbye.

I glance in my rearview only once to see him shove his hands in his pocket and turn towards his front door. I shake my head at him acting like a surly boy who didn't get his way.

He wanted me to spend the night but I refused. I was starting to get a little too comfortable there and that was the last thing I wanted to happen.

Tonight was already so unexpected. I knew it would be amazing. I knew he would fuck my brains out because he's done it before. But going to the trouble of not only cooking me dinner, but serving it, and being nervous about it. Then to carry me to a room filled with red roses, balloons, and candles. I was not expecting romance. I'm ashamed at how girly and giddy I'm feeling thinking about it.

I swear that orgasm he gave me has me all kinds of messed up in the head. Even so, I can't help but grin because this was the best night *ever*. I can finally check getting laid on Valentine's Day off my list and mark it as a success.

Time to focus on other things, like what's going to happen in three days when I get back. I was sure that tonight was the official one-and-done but now he's talking about dating. How long can we keep this up before one of us gets caught up in our feelings? With my luck, I know I'm going to be the one. I would have to be half dead not to get caught up in that man.

I shouldn't have agreed to any of this. I should have left it how it was that first time in his office. But no, that would have been too much like right. I had to go and agree to all of these damn one-and-dones. Now my dumb ass is about to jump out of the frying pan and right into the damn fire when I get back. I know I'm going to get my heart broken.

Maybe I shouldn't call him. Maybe I should just let it end like this—good like this. No mess, no drama, and no hurt feelings. I'll lose his number. I'll just go to Cancun, forget about him and it will really be done. That's what I'll do. I won't call him.

I'm not going to call. I am definitely, most certainly not going to call him.

But then what if not calling ends up being a mistake? What if he starts dating someone else to get back at me, falls in love, gets married, and has a bunch of kids? I'll be stuck watching that bitch live my life.

Hell no. I can't let that happen.

You know what, screw it, I'll call. I'm going to go for it. It'll probably end up being nothing anyway. Just a few fun little fucks. Nothing too serious. Who's to say I want kids. He probably doesn't even *like* kids.

But what if he does? He could end up being the one. Like he said, the possibilities are endless.

I'm going to call him as soon as I get back. Or maybe I should give it a day or two. Man, when did I become so indecisive? And why am I talking about marriage and kids? I'm only twenty-two. I'm letting this stupid day affect me. That's all it is.

Fucking Valentine's Day.

Gredin

ALONE IN my bedroom, I'm pleased with how the evening went. I sit on the side of the bed that still has the shape of Nichole's body imprinted on the sheets, looking at her number on my phone. What in the hell have I just gotten myself into telling her to call me when she got back from Cancun? It's all been fun and games so far, but if I keep this up, it's going to get serious.

I should just let her go. I know she's going to be trouble. She's been nothing but trouble since the day I met her.

Good trouble. Great trouble. Amazing trouble.

I look around the room with roses all over the place and the few balloons she didn't take hanging from the ceiling. I've opened up a can of worms with this shit. She liked it. She clearly wants romance so I'm going to have to keep it up. It's a guarantee now that I've suggested dating her.

Unfuckingbelievable. What happened to one-and-done? What happened to animalistic fucking and ducking? What happened to just helping a virgin out for Valentine's Day?

"Nothing too serious," she said. "Just looking to get laid by an older guy," she said.

Yeah, that's what the fuck she said, but that's not what's happening and it's my own damn fault because I keep going back for more. Why can't I get enough of this girl? How does she have me by *both* of my balls?

The chocolate sauce still sitting on the nightstand catches my eye. Remembering how it felt to have her lick that off them answers that question.

Fuck, she was amazing. Feisty as hell, but soft and so responsive. Jesus. She just ticks all the right boxes. Not just sexually. It's the way she moves, the way she smells, and the crazy shit that comes out of her mouth that keeps me laughing.

Damn, I'm getting too caught up in her.

I need to figure this shit out. She's going to be gone for three days. By then, I'm sure I'll forget all about her.

What if she forgets about me?

Why did that have to pop into my head? I don't need to start feeling any more territorial about her than I already do. I look at her number again, resisting the urge to call and see if she made it home okay.

Fuck this shit. I'm turning into a damn pussy. I need to delete the thing and be done with her once and for all. My finger hovers over the delete button, fighting with myself on whether or not I should do it. Before I can decide one way or the other, a message pops up on the screen.

NICHOLE: I made it home safe and sound.

I have to stop myself from laughing as my thumbs fly over the keys, answering her text.

> GREDIN: What makes you think I was worried?

> NICHOLE: I could feel you staring at the phone contemplating calling me from all the way over here.

Shit!

> GREDIN: You're feisty again. I like that.
> NICHOLE: Let's see how you'll like it when I get back. You're going to have to fuck a lot out of me.

I grin while reading what she wrote.

> NICHOLE: Stop with the cocky grin. You're still an asshole. I have to go. Dericka says I'm hers for the rest of the night.
> GREDIN: Please tell me you're not fucking her.
> NICHOLE: Not a chance. I'm all fucked out. Plus, I'm also strickly dickly from now on. Which is a good thing because I'm into yours.
> GREDIN: I'll be sure to make it worth your while. Goodnight, baby.
> NICHOLE: xoxo

I smirk at the hugs and kisses. I can almost hear her calling me an asshole for doing it.

Giving up the charade, I put her number on my speed dial and give it a ringtone so I'll know it's her when she calls. If she doesn't call me in three days, I'll call her. No doubt, I'm going to fucking call her, and I'll call every day after that.

I let out an indignant breath as I toss in the towel and concede.

Nichole Adams may have won the fight but I'm getting the prize.

If it's romance she wants then that's what she'll get. I promised to enjoy these flowers for her while she's gone, but when she returns, I'll buy her every damn flower she can think of. I'll get her a whole damn field of flowers if she wants it. And come this time next year this will be *our* bed. We won't be spending Valentine's Day in it. I'll take her somewhere that's much more worthy of her. Valentine's Day will be our day.

Of course, this all depends on if I play my cards right and win her over. Lucky for me, I have a whole year to stack the deck in my favor.

I don't plan on losing.

The End

Looking for another love story?
Have you read this office romance?

Sweet Surrender
Excerpt

FEEL A draft from my open office door and I glare at it to see who the hell's interrupting my private meeting. I'm about to let them have it until I see a young girl, no more than twenty standing in the doorway. Her hair's the first thing that catches my eye. It's light brown with streaks of blonde that look like sunbeams in her hair. It's pinned back in what looks to be a low bun so I can't tell the length. My admiration for it turns to fury when I remember her ass is in my office unannounced.

"Who are you?" I demand to know. "And what are you doing barging in on my meeting?"

Her mouth falls open and her eyes widen. It looks like she's struggling to think of something to say. How did she even get in here? This is the second time some college-age girl has crossed my path.

"Where the hell is Paris?" I ask her. She was supposed to prevent all interruptions. How this girl got past her is beyond me. She's obviously an employee of mine, but not a competent one. Everyone knows not to barge into my office. "How much of my conversation did you hear?"

Her refusal to answer my questions has just pissed me off and I let my barely checked temper get the better of me. I round my desk getting ready to rip her a new one before she holds up a legal-sized white envelope as an offering to me.

"Reed, hold on a minute," Lyle tells me as I move to take the envelope, but of course I ignore him.

I don't have the patience for this bullshit. I snatch the envelope from her hand and she runs out of my office as fast as her legs can take her.

"What the fuck was that about?" I ask Lyle.

"Her name's Reagan Montgomery."

"So? I don't give a damn who she is." Her not answering me felt like a goddamn dismissal.

"You really should give a damn. She goes to Walden University."

"Again, so?"

"Reagan's part of the outreach employment program. The one you were so hell-bent on starting there last year in your brother's honor."

"What in the hell are you talking about? You're full of shit. She seemed perfectly normal."

That program was designed to help physically and mentally disabled people gain on-the-job training and possible employment.

"Oh, she *is* perfectly normal. She's great, in fact."

"Says you. And aren't you supposed to be gay? I thought you people didn't notice shit like that."

"Well, aren't you itching for all kinds of discrimination lawsuits today."

"Will you just spit it out already. Why is she in the program?"

"She's deaf."

Shit!

AFTER GETTING my brain eaten three times, I give up playing the zombie attack game I accidentally downloaded when I was supposed to be preparing for my morning meeting and turn off my phone. Some commotion outside has me looking out the window. Two cars vying for the last parking space in front of the building catches my attention. The drivers are out of their cars pushing and shoving each other in the middle of traffic and there's a symphony of horns trying to get them to move. I sense someone approaching so I turn my head wondering who's interrupting me already. They could at least have the decency to wait until I've been here for more than an hour.

Fuck me, it's her. I was so caught up in the fight outside I didn't even hear her come in. Her face fills with apprehension and I can see that I've scared her again when she takes a step back. She's too far to read my lips so I move toward her before she can run, but I'm a second too late and she takes off.

"Miss Montgomery, wait. I'm not going to hurt you."

I call out to her in vain, knowing that she can't hear me. I catch her right before she goes out. My momentum almost runs her over before I catch myself with the door. She's frantic. I know she's having a panic attack, I used to have them as a kid. I spin her around to look at her. She drops the envelope and the phone she was carrying clatters on the marble floor. Grabbing her wrists, I pin them to the wall to stop her nails from trying to claw through my shirt. I try to get her to look at me, to see I'm not angry with her. I realize too late the position we're in and that it might be saying the opposite to her, especially when she can't hear my words.

What the fuck do I do now? I should let her leave but I know once I do, I'll never see her again, as scared as she is. Her fear is sending me right into predatory mode and fuck if my Dom doesn't show up soon after. This battle of wills is turning me on and pissing me off at the same damn time. I press my lips to hers in a last-ditch effort to subdue her and she freezes. Her whole body becomes rigid with the exception of her mouth. Her lips are moving with mine. Fuck, she's kissing me back. I can't help but moan at the softness of her lips. She pulls back a little to catch her breath before leaning in again kissing me this time. Jesus, she's into it, and I fucking like that.

Remembering that she's not my sub but a damn employee who can now very well sue me for sexual harassment, I take a step back and let her go. She stands completely still with her hands right where I left them. Her obedience is pushing all the right Dom buttons. It takes everything in me not to rush her again. I need her to stop being so submissive before I take her over to my desk and fuck the hell out of her. I gesture for her to lower her arms and watch as they move down to rest at her sides. She doesn't do anything else. Fuck, is she waiting for me to instruct her? No, no, no, I need her to move. She's still afraid of me, that's all this is. *She's not a submissive.* I need to think of something else to do to turn this shit around.

In between my jacking off to her last night, I did manage to look up a few words to sign, and now that I've got her attention, I try to communicate with her. I make a letter A with my fist and circle the center of my chest to say I'm sorry. I've never been the type to apologize, but I don't mind signing it if it'll stop her from being so damn responsive to me.

Her body relaxes and she smiles at me as she comes alive. She starts to sign to me, but her hands are moving too quickly. My two-hour *YouTube* tutorial on American Sign Language didn't show them signing this fast. There's no way I can figure out what she's telling me.

Shit.

Read more: https://books2read.com/ httpsbooks2readcomubwogPa

In the mood for something sinful?

Sugar Daddy
Excerpt

"GOOD EVENING, Mr. Remington. Welcome back to the Radiance Hotel. I have your suite all set up and waiting."

"That's very efficient of you, Miss St. James."

"Will you be alone for the duration of your stay?"

"I will unless you decide to join me."

"My break is in an hour."

"I'll see you then."

"I'm looking forward to it."

She hands me my room card before moving back to her desk. A mischievous smile plays on her lips as she tries to pretend she doesn't notice my stare. She gets distracted by a coworker, and I leave her to work, going up to my suite to prepare for her visit.

I pass by the vending machines and can't help but remember the first time I saw her there.

"Stupid machine," she said in frustration, hitting one that was tucked away behind a corridor marked "Employees Only."

Her voice made me curious. I'd heard it once before, so I followed where it led, rounding the corridor and venturing into the restricted area. There she stood, just like I'd pictured her in my mind: long black hair that was pulled back in a slick, braided ponytail, and flawless brown skin. I only saw her profile as she worked the buttons on the machine, but I recognized her immediately.

She looked up at me. Her eyes were a warm shade of brown. Like the Tennessee whiskey I used to find myself at the bottom of...

I knew right then and there I wanted her and even chastised myself for it. She was maybe twenty-two if she was graduating. I had ten years on her already. The last thing she needed was me fucking her up. It took everything I had to walk away.

But as luck would have it, there she was, a week later at the vending machines of the hotel I was forced to stay in because my usual one was closed for renovation.

She wore the uniform of a black skirt and white blouse. She held what looked like a honey bun in one hand, and a crumpled-up dollar, which the machine was refusing to take for something to drink, in the other. I watched as it spat her money out again, rejecting it.

"Give me a freaking break," she said. "All I want is a damn bottle of peach tea. Is that too much to ask?"

She tried to straighten the dollar out by running it along the hard edge of the machine but it didn't work, so she hit the machine again with the palm of her hand like that would make the tea fall out.

My eyes were as fixated on her at that moment as my mind had been for the last week. The way her tits bounced when she hit that machine had me fighting to stop my hard-on. No chance in hell was I passing up another *opportunity to get her in my bed. I'd been kicking myself over walking away from her the first time.*

Moving toward her with the precision of a starving lion stalking its prey, I opened my wallet and grabbed a bill.

"Try this one."

Read more: https://books2read.com/sugardaddy

Other Books by Rebel

Dare to Love Again Trilogy

Off Limits
https://books2read.com/offlimitsDTLA
Insatiable
https://books2read.com/insatiableDTLA
Treasured
https://books2read.com/treasuredDTLA

Daddy's Girl
https://books2read.com/u/bzgNwZ

Baby, It's Cold Outside
https://books2read.com/u/mZa7qB

Box Set

Dare to Love Again
https://books2read.com/DTLAboxset
Find more: https://rebelwildbooks.com/

Want to know the latest happenings?

Join Rebel's Newsletter:
https://rebelwildbooks.com/newsletter

www.ingramcontent.com/pod-product-compliance
Lightning Source LLC
Chambersburg PA
CBHW022131170626
46808CB00002B/941